NO CHOICE FOR A LADY

The difference between Lord Harry Lifton, the Marquess of Sidmouth, and Lord James Otley, Viscount Clitheroe, was plain for Kate Richmond to see.

Lord Harry was as heartless as he was handsome, and as relentless in his pursuit of continual conquest as he was successful at getting what he lusted for.

On the other hand, Lord James was as completely honorable as he was perfectly predictable, and as thoroughly devoted as he was utterly undemanding.

Clearly, choosing which one to love should have been simple for Kate.

And so it was.

Shockingly simple. . . .

HEARTLESS LORD HARRY

by

Marjorie Farrell

A SIGNET BOOK

SIGNET
Published by the Penguin Group
Penguin Books USA Inc., 375 Hudson Street,
New York, New York 10014, U.S.A.
Penguin Books Ltd, 27 Wrights Lane,
London W8 5TZ, England
Penguin Books Australia Ltd, Ringwood,
Victoria, Australia
Penguin Books Canada Ltd, 10 Alcorn Avenue,
Toronto, Ontario, Canada M4V 3B2
Penguin Books (N.Z.) Ltd, 182–190 Wairau Road,
Auckland 10, New Zealand

Penguin Books Ltd, Registered Offices:
Harmondsworth, Middlesex, England

First published by Signet, an imprint of New American Library,
a division of Penguin Books USA Inc.

First Printing, September, 1993
10 9 8 7 6 5 4 3 2 1

This one is for my brother,
John Aloysius Farrell.
Thanks, Jack.
If it hadn't been for
sibling rivalry, I wouldn't
be writing fiction.

ACKNOWLEDGMENTS

Many thanks to:

John Langstaff and the Revels, who brought the "Oss" to America

Folklife Productions, whose film, *Oss! Oss! Wee Oss!* was invaluable to me

Steeleye Span, whose stirring rendition of the Padstow song can be heard on their recording "Tempted and Tried"

and most important of all, the people of Padstow.

1

February, 1813

"The Marquess of Sidmouth to see you, my lord. Shall I tell him you are still at breakfast?"

James Otley, Viscount Clitheroe, looked up from his plate of ham and eggs. "Harry? No, show him in, Hanes. He needs fattening up."

"Yes, my lord."

The viscount did not pause in his slow, methodical consumption of his breakfast. When the marquess entered, Otley's mouth was full of muffin, and he had to wave his friend in with his cup of tea.

Henry Lifton, better known to his friends as Harry, grinned and made his way to the table. There was a slight hesitation in his walk, and when he sat down he was careful to stretch his right leg out in front of him.

The viscount washed down the last of his muffin and grinned at his friend. "You have given up the damned stick then, Harry?"

"Yes, the doctor finally allowed it . . . nay, advised it. Said I was getting too dependent on it."

"And your lung?"

"Right as rain. Not all right, either of them, when there *is* rain," admitted the marquess with a laugh. "But his recommendation is to get back to normal."

"Well, I'd say you have been doing that! Your activity this Little Season was even more frenetic than before you left for Portugal."

"I have two years to make up for, James."

"I find it hard to believe that you were not charming the senoritas in Spain and Portugal."

"The senoras, James. It was as difficult to get past a duenna to a young woman as it was to breach the walls of Badajoz," the marquess replied lightly.

It was one of his rare references to the battle in which he had been wounded, and typical of all of them: flippant and dismissive. James, who was dutiful, had listened to his family's protests and not sought a commission. Harry, who was defiant, had run off to war despite his mother's plea that he was the head of the family and owed it to the Sidmouth line to remain at home. James, although he had followed the progress of the campaign religiously and had read of the devastating losses of this particular siege, had no way of knowing what it must have been like. Not, he was damn sure, like getting past a young girl's chaperon. But if Harry did not want to talk about it, he was not going to pry.

"*Do* have some breakfast, my friend," said James with friendly sarcasm.

"Thank you," Harry responded in the same tone. He had already filled his plate and was consuming great quantities of eggs and kippers. "A man could starve awaiting your invitation."

"It never fails to amaze me, Harry, how you can pack it away and never gain an ounce. While I—"

"While you pack it away and are beginning to strain your waistcoats."

The viscount quickly looked down to see if any buttons were in immediate danger of popping. They were not, of course, for despite his friend's teasing, he was not really overweight, just taller and more solid than the marquess. James was stocky, but had no extra flesh on him. In buckskins, however, with his light brown hair, blue eyes, and ruddy complexion, he looked more like a ploughman than a Corinthian. The marquess, on the other hand, who had inherited his black hair and brown eyes from his Welsh mother, was devastatingly attractive, whether his slender frame was clad in buckskins or the maroon superfine he wore today.

"I am not in need of a corset yet, Harry," protested James.

"Well, I have a proposal that will keep you out of one."

"Indeed," said the viscount, raising his eyebrows.

"I have a mind to go walking."

"Walking? This morning? Isn't it rather early in the day?"

"Not that kind of walking. I want to get out of London for a while and wondered if you would join me."

"In what exactly?"

"A few weeks wandering with knapsacks on our backs and all our responsibilities forgotten."

"With *your* knee?"

"It is no longer painful, James, only stiff. And it is precisely because of it that I want to do this. I need to strengthen the leg and the lung, for that matter. I am sick of rest and coddling. If I am done with forced marches, I need some activity to replace them."

"I would have thought your dancing attendance on every available young woman and widow this fall kept you in shape! Isn't being charming enough exercise for you?"

"James, James, do I detect a bit of envy in your voice?"

"As much concern as envy, Harry. You were bad enough before you left. But my dear fellow, did you have to charm little Miss Celeste Durwood and then abandon her for Lady Sidney? Have you ever been serious about a woman?"

"Never."

"It is high time you settled down, you know. Found a wife and set up your nursery."

"That is part of the reason for this little walking tour, James. I will need all the stamina I can muster to make it through this next Season. I do intend to find a wife; I know what I owe to the family, for my mother has reminded me enough. Not, my dear friend, that I see you rushing to the altar."

James reddened. "The family has two females in mind. I shall choose between the Hargrave youngest or the Clement eldest."

"Nice of them to give you a choice!"

"Harry, you know the Otleys always do their duty. And you and I . . . we are very different. You can charm any woman from six to sixty, while I . . . I prose on and bore them to death."

"Now, James, we have talked of this before. You are most certainly not dull, but serious—someone to be relied on. A little too straitlaced, perhaps, but what else can one expect of an Otley! But come, will you go with me?"

"Just where were you planning to walk?"

"I had first thought of the South Downs Way, but that would be too easy. I have a longing for hills and dales. And your family has an estate in Yorkshire. What if we start there and work our way south?"

"When did you intend to start?"

"In two weeks."

"Two weeks! We will still be in February."

"Yes, the season of snowdrops and early daffodils."

"And late snowfalls."

"What of it. Actually, it would be a pleasure to be wet and cold after the heat and dust of Portugal."

"Are you sure you are strong enough for this?" Despite his teasing about the marquess's romantic activity, James had been worried about him in the fall. He had only regained some of the weight he had lost, and was blade-thin. And although his devil-may-care attitude toward women was characteristic, it had seemed to James that his frenetic activity was a direct result of the war. It was as though having recovered from a physical fever, he succumbed to an emotional one. For feverish activity was the best way to describe his progress through the Little Season. For all his charm and the protection his title gave him, more than one matron had begun to include Harry on the list of men for their daughters to avoid, a list that included arrant fortune-hunters and hardened libertines.

"James, I assure you I will not tumble down a fell or cough myself to death."

"All right, then, let us do it!"

2

K ate Richmond looked out her bedroom window, which overlooked the backyard of Richmond House. The early morning sun was shining, the sky was blue and cloudless, and the spring grass was a sparkling emerald green. She smiled as she watched Motley, their old tomcat, tremble with desire as he crouched, ready to pounce on the unaware warbler singing his heart out on the wall separating the yard from the pasture. She closed her eyes as Mott sprang, and hearing no more birdsong or pained shrieks, opened them again, relieved to see the cat perched on the wall. He was cleaning himself and looked disdainfully around as if to say "You thought I was after that bird and missed him? Why I was just aiming to sit down here on this warm stone. When I want to catch a bird, you'll know!" Kate turned away with a low chuckle and slipping her feet into well-worn brogues, went down to breakfast.

Her family was all there except for her mother who was already out on the hills keeping track of the lambing. Her father and her sister nodded their greetings to her from behind their books as she sat herself down to a bowl of porridge and fresh cream.

Spring was one of her favorite times in the dale, but was also one of the loneliest. Her mother was always tramping around from one shepherd's hut to another from early morning to teatime. Her sister and father . . . well, being buried in a book was not a seasonal failing for them, but in spring it was accompanied by an increase in energy and a desire to wander. They were not interested in tramping after sheep, however. They tramped off after holy wells and stone circles and chalk carvings in their quest to trace the roots of the old religions of Britain.

Kate sighed. She missed her brother even more this year than the last. She and Gareth had always been close, for they shared an affectionately ironic view of the rest of their family. Their father, Edward Richmond, a failed cleric and successful scholar had found in his older daughter a kindred spirit who had become equally obsessed by his studies. Their mother, Lady Elizabeth, to whom the family owed their financial stability, was dedicated to sheep-breeding, and always involved in trying to improve her stock. It was a warm and loving family, but sometimes its eccentricities drove her a little crazy.

Kate and Gareth were the practical ones. Lady Elizabeth was certainly practical, but only in the area of her obsession. She threw all her energy into sheep and hardly noticed her more immediate surroundings. Kate and her brother had no all-consuming interest. Both were concerned with the everyday running of Richmond House. They both helped their mother run the business, Kate by keeping the accounts and Gareth by taking over from time to time when Lady Elizabeth chose to accompany her husband on one of his research trips.

With Gareth, Kate could groan in despair over her mother's eccentricity or her sister's inability to see beyond her books. Even when her brother had been in the army, his letters had cheered her and made her feel that she was not alone. But these two years since his marriage had been hard for Kate. She visited Gareth and his wife at Thorne; he and Arden came to Sedbusk over the holidays, but it was not the same. He was as affectionate as ever, but his attention was naturally focused upon his wife. But no one's attention was focused upon her. Well, and why should it be, she would think, to pull herself out of the doldrums. I am lucky to have a loving family around me and responsibilities to keep me occupied.

On this particular morning she announced to her father and sister that she was off for a walk, for as she said, "It would be a shame to waste such a beautiful morning." Her father gave her an absentminded smile and Lynette muttered something about that being a good idea. Kate smiled and slipped out the door. For two people obsessed by what were essentially nature religions, it was ironic that her father and sister would rather spend their time indoors with their books than outside, up on the fells.

She headed up the path that ran straight up from the back of the house, intending to visit old Gabriel Crabtree, their head shepherd. Her legs and lungs were in excellent condition from all her tramping, and so she was hardly out of breath at all when she reached his hut. She peeked in, but the hut was empty, so she decided to continue up to the top of the scar and let the wind blow away her loneliness and discontent. But halfway up she met the old shepherd coming down with a dead lamb on his arm and his dog Benjamin driving a ewe before him.

"Good day to tha, lass."

"So we have lost one, Gabriel?"

"Aye. But I have one down in t'south pasture who needs a mother. Coom and help, will tha, lass?"

"Of course."

When they reached the south pasture, Gabriel had Benjamin drive the old ewe into a small pen in the corner. He laid the dead lamb on the ground and began, carefully and methodically, to skin it. Kate had seen him do this more than once, but it never ceased to amaze her that his hands, so big and heavy, could move with such dexterity and care. In minutes he had removed the fleece in one piece and held up what looked like a lamb coat, complete with leggings.

He whistled up Benjamin and pointed out the orphan. The dog nudged the forlorn-looking creature toward them, and Gabriel crooned soothingly as Kate helped him slip the little fellow, legs, tail and head, into the dead lamb's skin.

"There now, lad, let us see if tha new mother will take to tha."

He opened the gate to the enclosure and shooed the lamb in. For a moment the ewe just ignored him. Then, when the lamb took some steps in her direction, getting closer and closer, until he was almost next to her, she lowered her head as though getting ready to push him away. But then she caught the scent of his wool, which was, of course, the scent of her own dead lamb, and let him approach. She turned her body so he could nurse, and rubbed her muzzle contentedly along his back as he did so.

Kate felt tears rise, as they always did at such a scene.

"It always seems like a miracle to me," she said, with a trembling laugh.

"Oh, aye, lass, a miracle of short sight, strong scent, and stupidity."

"Now, Gabriel, you can't fool me. You are as happy as anyone when you save a lamb this way."

"Tha'rt reet, lass. Old as I am, I still feel a thrill when one of these old ewes lets a strange lamb nurse," admitted Gabriel. "Thank tha for tha help. I know I interrupted tha walk."

"No matter. I'll get out again this afternoon."

"I would not, if I were tha, lass. T'weather is going to turn. I think we are in for a little snow."

Kate looked up at the blue sky and over at Gabriel. "If it were anyone else predicting that, I should laugh at him, but you are always accurate. Although I am sure I don't know how."

"Well, it is old bones, lass. They be getting stiffer by the moment, and I can feel my arm aching reet now where I broke it two years ago."

"Will you be seeing Mother?"

"Oh, aye, I'll make sure her ladyship is home before the snow starts. I don't think it will be a long one, but I feel it will be a bad one."

3

"Pass me the cheese, James."

Harry sat with his back against a stone wall and basked in the warm sun. He gave a relaxed sigh and said, "This has been the best day of our whole trip."

James broke off a piece of cheese and passed it over. "We have one more bottle of cider. Do you want to split it?"

"Yes, I have quite a thirst after this morning's climb."

The two men had shed their coats and knapsacks and were stretched out, enjoying the sun which felt gentler, now that they weren't sweating and climbing up the fell.

"I must tell you, Harry, that I had my doubts about this idea of yours, but this has been a splendid week. And you have been able to keep up with me pretty well," he added teasingly.

"Keep up with you! Who was out of breath after two miles the first day?" replied Harry with mock outrage, tossing a large pebble in James's direction.

"All right, I admit it. We are both in better shape," admitted James. He looked over at Harry who had drunk the last drop of cider and had his face up to the sun. He had regained some color this week, thought James. And despite the stiffness in his knee, had had little trouble negotiating the hills. At the end of the day, the hesitation in his walk was a bit more pronounced, but by the first hour out in the morning it would almost disappear, and the walking staff Harry had brought for support was hardly needed.

His lung, on the other hand, worried James. While it was true that Harry didn't seem much more out of breath than he did, he had a tendency to fall into a short fit of coughing whenever they stopped. And occasionally James noticed him rubbing his lower back, as though trying to reach the site of his original wound. But when he questioned him, Harry laughed and said, "James, the doctors told me that taking a bayonet through the lung was bound to weaken it. The cough is nothing to worry about."

Nevertheless, James did worry and felt like a fussy old hen when he found himself admonishing Harry to put his coat back on if he was going to lean against cold and damp stones. Harry would only get annoyed and then when they were back on the path, walk faster as if to prove that he was in no way limited.

James smiled to himself as he thought of his friend's stubbornness. He settled himself against the wall, and within a few minutes, tired from the morning's exertion and relaxed by his meal, he fell asleep.

When he awoke, he was afraid he had slept overnight and into the next morning, a cold, gray, cloudy morning. The perfectly blue sky was now a mass of low hanging clouds. The sun was a memory. And the clouds seemed to be spitting out rain . . . no, snow. "It can't be snowing," he exclaimed.

"But it is," said Harry with a grimace as he pulled on his coat and slung his knapsack over his shoulders.

James shivered in his damp clothing as he pulled his own coat on. Neither of them had brought anything suitable for winter weather. They had spent most of their nights in local inns, so they had had no need. And now here they were, at the top of a fell, a few miles from the nearest town, and it felt like the middle of December.

"We'd better get started," urged Harry, picking up his walking staff. "Hawes is the closest town, and that is at least three miles away. I don't like the look of those clouds."

"Surely it is just a snow squall? They blow over quickly enough."

"I hope so, James."

Within half an hour they were both praying it was a

squall. The temperature seemed to have dropped twenty degrees or more, and the snow, which had started mixed with rain, was now coming down thick and fast. And they were walking into the wind. Which at least keeps our eyes on the path, thought James, as he struggled after Harry.

They managed to go a mile or so before they admitted to themselves that the storm was not blowing over, just blowing harder.

"Harry," James called.

Harry stopped and turned. His friend looked like a snow-covered bear. "What is it, James? We have to push on."

"We have to find shelter, Harry. This is madness."

"I agree we need shelter, James," said Harry sarcastically, "but do you see any?"

"I can't see bloody anything."

"So we must push on to Hawes."

"You don't have to sound so bloody superior, Harry. This is no joke."

"Believe me, I know. It is getting darker and I can hardly see my hand in front of my face, much less the path. But we must go on. I am afraid this snow is going to last all night."

"Do you want me to lead?"

"No, I am fine, James."

James thought they had gone another half mile before it happened, but they were going so slowly that it might well have been only a few hundred yards. He heard Harry curse and almost tripped over him as he caught up.

"God damn it. Bloody, bloody hell."

"What is it?"

"I've wrenched the bloody knee," Harry groaned, struggling to get back on his feet.

"Don't get up, you fool."

"I *have* to get up, James. I can't stay here. I'll freeze to death. Give me the staff."

James groped around on the path and found it. He grasped his friend by the arm and hauled him up.

"All right, all right." Harry was balancing himself on one leg. "Give me the staff and we'll go on." Harry took two steps and was on the ground again, cursing his knee, the snow, the bloody French and the even bloodier British.

"Here, give me your arm. I am going to carry you."

"Don't be ridiculous. You can't do that. Leave me here and go for help."

"Here? Here? We don't even know where *here* is!" James leaned down, and slinging his friend over his shoulder, grasped the staff and moved on. He had not realized how walking behind Harry had sheltered him from the wind and given him a little sense of what was in front of him. No wonder Harry had fallen. One couldn't see the path. One had to feel for it, and with feet like blocks of ice, that was hard to do.

James lost all sense of time as he stumbled slowly onward. At first Harry had been cursing him and demanding to be put down, but after his protests were completely ignored, he lay quiet. James thought he must have gone at least a mile and was wondering if he would be able to see the lights of the town. But perhaps they had passed it and were walking toward nowhere. All of a sudden the path turned and went downhill at the same time, and he stumbled. He was brought to his knees and Harry rolled off his shoulders with a groan. It felt good to give up the struggle, even if for only a moment. In fact, he was ready to give it up completely. They could huddle together for warmth; the snow would stop by morning, and the sun would come out and wake them. He was about to close his eyes when he realized that he was succumbing to the sleepiness that came with cold and snow.

"Harry! Are you all right?"

"Aside from being dropped like a sack of potatoes, yes, I think so. Look, James," he continued in a maddeningly rational voice, "this is not going to work. We must be almost to Hawes. I am sure there must be houses a few hundred yards from here. Leave me, and hurry on and get help."

"I'm not leaving you," protested James.

"You have to, or we will both freeze to death. Come on now, Jamie, it can't be far and I promise I'll wait for you right here," said Harry, trying for humor.

James smiled at the old nickname and Harry's coaxing tone. He sounded just like the ten-year-old boy who used to coax his best friend into trouble when they were at school.

"Maybe you are right," he admitted. "We must be near a farmhouse by now. But I am leaving you my coat," he added, struggling out of it and laying it over his friend's shoulders. "I will be moving, and you will need it more than I will."

Harry bit back his refusal and felt tears slip down his cheeks and freeze on their way down. It was just like Jamie to act with such kindness.

"Thank you, Jamie. And now the sooner you go, the sooner you'll come back."

"Now, don't move, Harry. I'll be back within the hour, I'm sure."

Harry was not going anywhere. Harry's knee was swollen and stiff. And Harry didn't want to go anywhere, anyway. He huddled under James's coat and gave in to the sleepiness his friend had fought off. He knew what it meant. By the time James got back—if James got back—he would be lying there, quite comfortably blanketed by snow, having painlessly frozen to death. But at least James might make it. He pillowed his head on his arm and muttered a curse at the arbitrariness of fate. He had survived Badajoz only to succumb to a snowstorm in Yorkshire? God's bloody balls.

4

James didn't know how many times he had fallen, gotten up, and forced himself to go on. If he had been alone, he would have lain where he fell. But he made himself get up, made himself go on, because of Harry. Harry was waiting for him. Harry would freeze to death if he didn't get help.

He almost didn't hear the dog. Or rather, he almost didn't believe he had heard a dog. The wind blew the sound away almost as soon as it occurred. He started shouting, and it seemed to him that the dog answered. He was going downhill now, at a stumbling run, and when he looked up at one point he thought he saw a light, thought he heard an answering shout. And then there was a lantern in his face and a dog dancing around his feet, and he let himself be led into a small hut.

"My God, lad, what art tha doing out on a night like this?"

James looked at his savior. Although maybe the black-and-white dog was his savior? No, Christ was his savior. That is what he and Harry had learned in school . . .

"Harry, I must get back to Harry," he mumbled, his lips and cheeks stiff with cold.

"Hurry? Hurry for what, lad? Tha'rt safe and warm now, thanks to Benjamin here. Ah, old lad, tha'rt a good old lad," crooned the old man to his dog.

"Harry, my friend Harry is out there on the fell side. We must go back for him."

The old man looked up, startled. "Soomone else out there with tha? How long since tha left him?"

"Less than a half hour, I think."

"I hope tha'rt reet. Coom, Benjamin. No, tha sit still by t'fire and I'll go out after tha friend."

"But you'll never find him," protested James. "And he's hurt, he can't walk. I must go with you."

"Nay, tha'll never find anything in t' storm. But Benjamin can. And I'll carry him back."

James looked more closely at his rescuer. He was tall and built like an oak, but he was also grizzled with age. "Are you sure you can carry him down?"

"How did he make it that far, lad, if he cannot walk?"

"I carried him the last mile or so."

"Well, if tha can do it, I shall. Coom, Benjamin. There is warm milk on t'stove. It is for t'lamb, but you may have some." And with that last cryptic announcement, the old man was gone and James was alone. Milk for the lamb? Then he noticed the basket by the fire where a woolly shape lay curled asleep. The basket looked as if it had seen years of similar use. James apologized silently to the lamb and stumbled over to the stove, where he poured himself some milk. He took a great gulp and then almost spit it out. From the strong taste he guessed it was sheep's milk. He managed to get it down, together with a few crusts of bread from the table. He didn't think the old man would mind.

He had almost dozed off, despite his anxiety, when the barking aroused him. He opened the door and saw a giant white misshapen figure approaching, which resolved itself into the old shepherd with Harry slung over his shoulder.

"Oh, thank God," said James as he stumbled forward to help.

"Lay him doon on t'old cot," ordered the shepherd.

"Be careful of his right knee," cautioned James, as the old man and he put Harry down.

"Oh, aye, it does feel a bit swollen."

"He wrenched it a mile or so back, and he had only recovered from having a ball removed."

"A soldier?"

"Yes, he was on the Peninsula."

"Well, he is a lucky one. A bit longer and tha'd been a

dead soldier," said the shepherd, shaking Harry gently. "Wake up, lad. We must get something doon tha throat."

It took a few minutes to shake Harry awake. He felt himself being shaken, but did not want to open his eyes. Could one open one's eyes once one had died, he wondered. When he finally decided to try, he saw a huge, dirty creature leaning over him. He smelled of smoke and dog and wool. The whole room was smoky, in fact, and Harry wondered if he were waking up in Hell. Christ, I'd have thought my time in Spain and Portugal was hell enough for any sinner, he said to himself. Then he saw James's face anxiously peering down. "No, no, not you, Jamie. Why, there cannot be any Otleys in Hell. They are too damned dull and dutiful."

"Hell? Is that where tha thinks tha art, lad?" The old man laughed long and hard. "Na, that is a good one. No. Tha'rt in Sedbusk."

"Then we made it, Jamie?"

"Yes, Harry, we made it thanks to Mr. . . . ?"

"Crabtree. Gabriel Crabtree."

"Mr. Crabtree and his dog Benjamin."

Having heard his name, Benjamin came over to the cot and shoved his nose into Harry's hand.

"Can tha feel tha hands and feet, lad?"

Harry winced. "I am beginning to and almost wish I couldn't."

"Tha'rt all reet, then. It will be painful, but it is better than no feeling at all and losing fingers and toes after. Tha'rt both very lucky. Na get soom sleep. Tha can lay on t'floor," he said to James. "I'll get tha a blanket."

"But where will you sleep?"

"In t'chair. Don't worry about me." And Gabriel provided James with an old sheepskin to lie on and a blanket to cover himself, and then, settling into the chair, fell asleep almost instantly.

James was awakened the next morning by the sun. It was hard to get up, as uncomfortable as the floor was, for he was tired right down to his bones. But he dragged himself over to the door and opened it onto a beautiful morning. Gabriel Crabtree came around the corner of his house at that moment. "Good morning to tha, lad."

"I can't believe that last night ever happened. Except there is the snow."

"Aye. But it will be gone by t'afternoon. How art tha feeling?"

"Tired and stiff."

"And tha friend? I heard him coughing during t'night."

"I didn't, but then, I slept like the dead," said James. "I hope he has not developed an inflammation."

"Well, I intend to get tha both down to the big house this morning. Tha'll be more comfortable there, and if tha needs a doctor, t' missus will summon one."

5

Harry did have a cough and felt feverish to James, although he denied it vehemently. The swelling in his knee had gone down, but it was still painful for him to walk, so Gabriel supported him on one side while he used his walking stick on the other, and they made it slowly down the path.

Both James and Harry were surprised by their first sight of Richmond House. They had expected a typical Yorkshire farmhouse, and instead saw a respectable-size country home. Gabriel knocked at the front door, and after a few moments wait, it was opened by an angel. Or so it seemed to James. The sun was behind them and illuminated a tall, ethereal-looking young woman with hair so light it was almost silver. She smiled at Gabriel which made her look even more beautiful if that was possible. James had never felt solider, clumsier, or duller, as he heard Harry introduce himself and comment upon how they seemed to have gone from Hell to Heaven overnight.

He will be charming on his deathbed, thought James resentfully. Here he is, limping and exhausted, and he can still play the rake. Then Harry fell into a fit of coughing, and James was ashamed of himself. It had always been so: Harry the lady's man and James his foil. But it had never rankled as much, he thought, as they were ushered in by the angel.

"You sound dreadful, sir. Let me get my sister."

"That is Miss Lynette Richmond," said Gabriel proudly. She is the beauty of the family."

In a minute the angel was back with her sister, a small,

attractive young woman with curly brown hair and gray eyes and a take-charge air about her.

"I am Kate Richmond. My sister tells me that Gabriel rescued you from the storm last night?"

Harry was still bemused by Lynette, so James answered. "Yes. We were caught up on the fell, and Harry was unable to walk. Mr. Crabtree saved our lives, I am sure."

"Na then, lad, tha saved thaself. Had tha not pushed on, Benjamin would never have found tha."

"Well, whoever is the hero," said Kate briskly, "it does seem that your friend here is a bit feverish and should be put to bed. It is Janie's day off, so I will get you settled in the spare room. Gabriel, can you carry this gentleman up the stairs?"

Harry protested, but that only set him off coughing again, so Gabriel just scooped him up and followed Kate up the stairs while James watched.

"Would you like to come into the parlor, Mr. . . . ?"

"Otley. James Otley."

Lynette led him into a cozy room where a fire was blazing. "Come, sit down, and when Kate returns, we will have some tea. What were you doing up on the fell?"

"Harry and I were on a walking trip. We fell asleep on what seemed a warm spring day and awoke in a snowstorm."

"It can happen in the dales," Lynette said. "And I have heard of men dying of exposure, so you were both lucky."

"They certainly were," said Kate from the door. "But I think we should call the doctor for your friend."

"You don't really think it is serious?" asked James, rising from his seat.

"No, no, he is just warm, not burning up. But I don't like the sound of his cough."

"He was wounded last year at Badajoz, and one lung is weak as a result," explained James. "But his doctors said he was fully recovered."

"He keeps insisting he is fine. But if he has a weak lung, an inflammation could too easily set in. But do not look so worried. I am keeping him in bed and calling the doctor more as a preventive measure. How are you feeling after your ordeal?"

"Tired and stiff but otherwise unharmed. I cannot thank you enough for taking us in like this."

"Nonsense! Now, let me get us some tea. Lynette, will you help me?"

James leaned back in his chair and drifted off almost immediately after the sisters had left. He was awakened by the rattle of the tea tray and tried to rouse himself.

"I think we should have put you to bed too, Mr. Otley," said Kate with a smile.

"No, no, I slept well last night, truly I did."

"On Gabriel's floor?"

"It was warm and safe, and it was a relief to let myself go. I had been very tempted to fall asleep in the snow."

"I have heard of that phenomenon," said Kate. "You were very lucky, for that is exactly the way people freeze to death."

"Well, it would be a peaceful way to die, from what I experienced. I can understand why men give in to it."

James drank his tea and devoured the warm scones that Kate had brought out and looked at the elder Miss Richmond as much as he could without being impolite. He wondered about the family. "Richmond" didn't immediately sound familiar to him, but judging from the size of the house and the cultured tones of the sisters, Mr. Richmond must surely be a gentleman.

"Now, Mr. Otley, I insist you go upstairs, too. I have had Gabriel make up a bed next to your friend, and you should be fairly comfortable."

James didn't even attempt an argument. Despite the tea and scones, or perhaps because of them, he felt sleepy and was only too happy to proceed upstairs, where after placing his hand on Harry's forehead and satisfied that his friend was not running a high fever, he lay down on the cot, pulled up the covers, and fell immediately asleep.

Downstairs the two sisters discussed their guests.

"They seem like gentlemen, Kate. Did you recognize their names?"

"No, but why should we? We have neither of us been to London in years. But I agree that from their speech I would assume they are from good families—perhaps even from the nobility, although they did not introduce themselves that way. But Harry of the weak knee and lung, good family or not, is obviously a lady's man," she added with contempt.

"Now, Kate, why do you say that?"

"Because he was trying to flirt with you between coughs, Lynette."

"I didn't really notice," her sister confessed. "I was just so surprised to see them here at all."

"Well, I'll send Jake down for Dr. Crowe. But when this Harry is allowed downstairs, I want you to take care," her sister said protectively.

The doctor arrived two hours later and had to awaken his patient to examine him.

"Your knee is only slightly swollen, but I would use a stick to keep your full weight off it for a few days," he told Harry after he gently probed his leg.

"Just when I had got rid of the damned thing!"

"Oh, I don't think this has set you back that much," the doctor reassured him. "Now let me listen to that lung. Cough."

Harry coughed obediently and that cough set off a mild fit of coughing.

"Hmm. Again."

"Again? I am trying to stop coughing."

"Once more, lad, and I'll be finished."

Another cough on demand. This time Harry was lucky and it ended with that.

"I don't hear any signs of inflammation. It is obvious the lung was weakened permanently by your injury, but although I am sure the cough is irritating, there seems to be nothing to worry about. It will subside in a few days. You were very lucky, sir. Another few hours in the snow, and my diagnosis might well have been pneumonia."

"Another few hours in the snow and your diagnosis

would more likely have been 'frozen to death,' " Harry joked. "When can I get up?"

"You may get up for tea today, if you feel like it. But I would not plan any strenuous activity for at least a week."

"Well, that ends our walking tour, James."

James didn't answer because James was still asleep. He had slept through the doctor's visit, and it looked as though he was going to sleep the day away.

"I will leave you a cough syrup that should give you some relief. Keep off the knee as much as you can. Luckily I leave you in good hands here."

"The Richmonds have been more than kind," agreed Harry. "And it should not be too hard to stay quiet if I can have that blond angel attending me."

"Miss Richmond? Oh, aye, she is beautiful, but you had better wish that Miss Kate has the care of you. Miss Richmond is more likely to let the tea stew and the toast burn while she is finishing up a chapter," the doctor said and laughed.

"That ethereal creature, a bluestocking?"

"A scholar, yes."

"And Miss Kate Richmond?"

"She is the practical one—keeps the accounts. Manages the household. Now, she would make a wonderful helpmate for a man," teased the doctor.

"For a man who is looking for one."

"You had better not be looking for anything else," warned the doctor. "The Richmonds are a respected family here in Wensleydale."

Harry yawned. "No need to warn me. I am a gentleman, and moreover, I am too tired for anything but a mild flirtation with the angel."

"Aye, I thought you might both be gentlemen. Well, take the medicine I leave you and my advice on the knee. I will stop in again tomorrow." As he closed the door behind him, Dr. Crowe chuckled to himself. He would like to be there when Mr. Harry Lifton tried to flirt with Miss Richmond. Most likely, she would not even notice! And his patient seemed like a man unused to having his charms ignored.

6

Neither man made it down to tea, but James awoke shortly after, and having splashed some water on his face and brushed his hair as best he could with his fingers, left Harry to sleep the clock around and made his way downstairs.

He heard voices in the parlor and gently knocked on the door as he opened it slowly and peered in.

"Come in and meet our parents, Mr. Otley," said Kate with a welcoming smile. "We have just had our tea, but I will get you something if you are hungry."

James did not want to trouble her, but on the other hand, had not eaten since early morning. "I hate to be a bother," he said hesitantly, "but I am a bit hungry."

"Of course. Lynette, you do the introductions, and I will bring Mr. Otley a tray."

Lynette coolly introduced James to her father, Edward Richmond, and her mother, Lady Elizabeth. Edward Richmond was a short, stocky man with a receding hairline. Lady Elizabeth was a tall, thin, gray-haired woman with the same violet-blue eyes as her eldest daughter. It was clear that Miss Kate took after her father, and Lynette after her mother. When Kate returned with the tea, and they began to converse, it became clearer however, that the resemblances were only physical. Although Lady Elizabeth was blunter, she and Kate had a practical air about them and tended to dominate the conversation. Miss Richmond, on the other hand, seemed more like her father, quiet, indeed a trifle distracted, as though both their thoughts and energy were only partially engaged in the conversation.

"I understand from Dr. Crowe that you are a scholar, Miss Richmond," commented James after there was a lull in the conversation.

"I am my father's assistant, if that is what you mean, Mr. Otley." James would have expected any woman accused of bluestocking tendencies to blush and downplay her interests, but Miss Richmond only announced them quite matter-of-factly. "He is writing an investigation of the pagan religions in Britain and the way they have survived even after the arrival of Christianity. I aid him with his research and help edit his book."

"You are far too modest, my dear. She is an excellent writer and scholar in her own right, and has contributed two chapters," announced Mr. Richmond proudly.

Kate watched with amusement as Mr. Otley obviously struggled to find the right compliment and almost laughed aloud as he made the obvious one.

"Your daughter is so very lovely that one would never guess she was also intelligent." Immediately as he said the words, James realized how they had come out. "Not," he stammered, making it even worse," that I would have thought her . . . "

"Dull, Mr. Otley?" Kate immediately regretted her impulse to tease, for Mr. James Otley was blushing as hotly as one would have expected Lynette to do.

"Uh, no, that is not at all what I meant."

Kate took pity on him. "Forgive me, Mr. Otley. You are not the first man to be surprised that beauty and intelligence can exist simultaneously in a woman."

James had avoided looking at Miss Richmond all this time. He turned to apologize for the clumsiness of his compliment, expecting her to be at least a little bit flustered. But she was sitting there calmly, as though she were merely an observer and not the one being spoken of. She merely nodded at James as he brought his apology to a somewhat incoherent conclusion and poured him another cup of tea.

"And what are your chapters about, Miss Richmond?" asked James, after a few gulps of tea.

"I am particularly interested in the surviving customs that have to do with ensuring fertility."

Luckily James had swallowed his tea, for otherwise he would have disgraced himself further and choked on it.

"How very, uh, interesting," was all he could manage. What he was thinking was, how very odd for an angelic-looking young woman to be investigating crude country customs. His mother would have been horrified had either of his sisters even used the word "fertility."

"It is fascinating," continued Lynette, oblivious to James's discomfort. "Most people think the customs have only to do with ensuring the harvest, but there is a definite link between celebrating the earth's fecundity and the union of men and women, or so some scholars believe."

Miss Richmond sounded just like one of his Oxford tutors in the lecture hall, conveying some dry bit of history. From the expression on his face, her father was quite proud of her.

"Tell me, Mr. Otley," said Lady Elizabeth, changing the subject, to James's great relief, "were both you and your friend in the military?"

"No, Lady Elizabeth. I had family obligations. I suppose I should introduce myself more accurately," he added diffidently. "I *am* James Otley, but I am also the Viscount Clitheroe."

"So we should be calling you Lord Clitheroe?" said Kate.

"And your friend, is he plain Mr. Lifton?" asked Lady Elizabeth.

"Actually, he is Harry Lifton, Marquess of Sidmouth."

"I think I might have known his mother. Was she Maria Radnor?"

"Yes, I believe so."

"She was a lovely girl. Married the marquess, to the despair of her family. He was very wild in those days. But he had great charm. I am sorry to hear he is dead."

"Yes, Harry inherited the title five years ago."

"And went off to the Continent anyway?" Kate asked.

"It was very upsetting to his mother," admitted James.

"But he takes after his father, perhaps?"

"Harry has always been a bit on the wild side."

"And you are not," observed Lady Elizabeth, who, impatient with conventional politeness, always spoke her mind. "You are a dutiful son."

James was going to protest, but then, why protest what must be construed as a compliment. Only, somehow, dutifulness and steadiness seemed dull compared with Harry's inherited wildness and charm.

"It is admirable, Lord Clitheroe," added Kate, "when after weighing one duty against another, a man chooses the less glamorous of the two."

James appreciated her obviously sincere compliment, but wished that it had come from the lips of Miss Richmond. But given her unorthodox interests, she would more likely respond to Harry's devil-may-care brand of courage.

"Thank you, Miss Kate."

After tea the family went their separate ways: Mr. Richmond and Lynette to his study, Kate and her mother to go over the week's accounts. James was invited to take advantage of the library or to stay in front of the parlor fire as long as he wanted.

He did find a book that interested him and managed to read for an hour before dozing off again. He got himself upstairs and let himself into their room quietly. He walked over to where Harry lay fast asleep and gently felt his friend's forehead. It felt cool, thank God, and the doctor's syrup must have worked, for he was not coughing.

"You'll be up and about tomorrow, charming the Misses Richmond, no doubt," whispered James, much relieved that Harry's health had only been weakened, not seriously damaged by his wounds.

7

The next morning Harry was awake at sunrise. He stretched his legs carefully, but aside from a slight twinge in his bad knee, he felt fine. He took a deep breath, which caused a few coughs, but nothing more than he usually did early in the morning. James stirred at the noise but did not wake, and Harry quietly got out of bed and limped over to the chair where his clothes lay. They smelled smoky from the night in Gabriel's hut, but there was nothing he could do about it, so he pulled them on. Grasping his walking staff, which made him feel ridiculous, but which did, he had to admit, keep weight off his knee, he went downstairs.

He heard noise from the back of the house and went toward what he guessed was the kitchen. He had guessed correctly and opened the door on a small, plump, gray-haired woman who was stirring a large pot of porridge on the stove.

"Good morning," Harry said.

"Good morning to tha, lad. Tha must be the military gentleman that Dr. Crowe told George about."

"George?"

"My husband. He was in t'pub for a pint when t'doctor came in."

"Word spreads fast in Yorkshire," said Harry with a smile.

"Aye, in a small place like Hawes it does indeed. Now, tha should sit down and rest thaself, lad."

"I appreciate your concern, Mrs. . . . ?"

"Pratt. But tha can call me Janie."

"Janie. But I need to walk a little or the knee will stiffen up. I thought I would go out for a short stroll. Is there time before breakfast?"

"Aye, tha has ten minutes or so."

Harry gave her his most charming smile and slipped out the back door into the yard, leaving Janie wondering if she were twenty years younger, would she have followed right behind.

The snow was gone except for a few small patches up on the scar, and it was obviously going to be a glorious spring day. Harry took a deep breath of the clear air, but did not cough at all, only feeling the familiar pull from the bayonet scar. He hated the feeling, hated anything that reminded him of the day he was wounded, and so he moved on, keeping his memories behind the locked door he refused to open. As he rounded the corner of the house, he saw a tall, gray-haired woman coming down the path. She was dressed in an old wool gown with a cloak thrown over her shoulders to keep off the early morning chill. He took her to be a local farmer's wife.

"Good morning, Lord Sidmouth," she called out, and Harry started in surprise.

"Good morning, Mrs. . . . ?"

"Richmond. Lady Elizabeth Richmond," the woman replied, holding out her hand. "You look very like your mother."

"Are you some sort of witch that you know both my name and my mother?" Harry asked quizzically.

"Lord Clitheroe revealed your identity to us last night."

"Ah, James. I should have guessed. And you knew my mother?"

"We were presented the same Season. A lovely girl, Maria. Is she well? But enough of ancient history," continued Lady Elizabeth, not waiting for an answer. "Let me see you walk."

"I feel ridiculous with this staff, but the doctor prescribed it for a few days," said Harry as they walked up the path together.

"And your fever?"

"Gone."

"You were lucky Gabriel found you, my lord. Even Yorkshiremen who should know better have died up in the Pennines."

"And thank God for James's strong back."

"A good friend, Lord Clitheroe."

"From my school days."

"And yet you seem very different."

"As unlike as chalk and cheese," admitted Harry. "James's family is very sober and conventional, and he is a devoted son and heir. While my family . . . well, you know that my mother ran off with the wild Marquess of Sidmouth and scandalized society."

"And are you as wild as your father, my lord?"

"I have managed to avoid some of his excesses, Lady Elizabeth. I have fought no duels. Instead, I went to the Peninsula to fight the French."

"And women?"

"I am very discreet—both in my dealings with the ladies and in conversations like this one."

"A neat sidestep, lad. Come, we had better turn back. I am sure Janie has breakfast ready."

Breakfast was indeed ready and everyone, including James, was seated when they went in.

"Harry, I was wondering where you were and how you were," his friend cried.

"Feeling almost normal, James. Except for a bit more stiffness in the knee and an occasional cough, I feel completely recovered."

James's face was beaming, and Kate, who had been observing the two men, thought what a nice man Lord Clitheroe seemed to be. A nice man and a courageous one. What Lord Sidmouth was remained to be seen. But she suspected she had his measure. He was likely a handsome charmer who broke hearts right and left.

Harry was introduced to Mr. Richmond and then turned to Lynette. "I believe I need a proper introduction to your daughter, sir. Daughters," he corrected himself, with barely a glance in Kate's direction.

Introductions were made, and after a cool smile, Miss Lynette Richmond went right back to her breakfast. Harry found her lack of response challenging, and determined to get a blush out of her, if not a kiss, before they left. Of course, he'd clearly have to get by her watchdog sister. A not unattractive girl, but bossy and officious, he'd wager.

"Miss Richmond and her father are scholars, Harry," James informed him.

Harry turned to Kate and politely congratulated her, thinking to himself that it made sense that she was a blue-stocking.

"Oh, no, not me, Lord Sidmouth," said Kate, with a twinkle in her eye. "Lynette is the scholar in the family. I merely have a good head for mathematics."

Harry turned to Lynette. He found it hard to believe that such an ethereally beautiful woman would spend her time grubbing around with books. He decided it made her a more interesting challenge, however. Could he distract her from her studies long enough to start a mild flirtation, he would not mind being holed up on a sheep farm for a few days.

"Tell me, sir," asked Harry, addressing his host, "do you by any chance have a cousin or nephew who served with Wellington? I was in Portugal with a Captain Gareth Richmond."

Before her father had a chance to answer, Kate broke in. "You knew my brother? What an amazing coincidence."

"Yes." With the enthusiastic look on her face, Harry thought, Miss Kate Richmond was really quite attractive. "I believe he sold out shortly thereafter?"

"He was obliged to come home for two reasons," Kate's mother answered. "To run the farm for us while we were in Wales on a research trip of my husband's. And to assume his title. Gareth is now the Marquess of Thorne."

"Then you must have been the Lady Elizabeth Tremayne before you wed Mr. Richmond?"

"Yes, I ran off with him just as your mother ran off with her marquess," replied Lady Elizabeth with a smile. "My brother had no children, and so he designated Gareth his heir."

"Your son was an excellent officer. We were sorry to lose him."

"Well, we were overjoyed to get him back unharmed," said Kate without thinking. "Oh, I am sorry. That sounds as though we only care about our own."

"Nothing to apologize for, Miss Richmond. After all, I am also one of the lucky ones who made it home."

"Well," said Lady Elizabeth briskly, "I must be off. Perhaps if you feel up to it, Lords Clitheroe and Sidmouth, you might want to walk into Hawes. Kate was planning to go in, weren't you, dear?"

"Yes, Mother. I do have some errands."

"And Lynette, why don't you take a holiday and go with your sister," added Mr. Richmond, to his wife's surprise and secret approval. Her girls met very few men in the dales, and she did not want to let an opportunity go to waste. But Edward was usually aware only of what was going on in his books, not at his breakfast table!

Lynette looked up in surprise. "Are you sure, Father? I thought you wanted me to edit those last few pages."

"I, er, have a few changes I decided to make, my dear. No, you go on and enjoy yourself."

8

The four of them gathered at the front of the house an hour after breakfast.

"It is only a mile, my lord," Kate said to Harry, "but I hope that is not too much for you."

"I assure you, although the staff looks a bit odd, it gives me adequate support. And the whole purpose of this walking trip was to strengthen my leg, not pamper it. I would hate to lose through inactivity what I have gained over the past week."

They set off down the road four abreast until they came to a stile. "If we climb over here," announced Kate, "we can go across the small pasture. Otherwise," she apologized, "it is more than a mile by road."

Harry hung back so that James was nearest Kate and was the one to hand her over the stile. Then he clambered over and turned back to offer Lynette his hand. He concentrated all his attention on his hand touching hers, but she took it matter-of-factly and let it go immediately, and Harry could feel no magnetism between them at all.

The path through the pasture was narrow, and so they walked two by two, Kate chattering away to James in front of them. The elder Miss Richmond was silent, and Harry could think of no opening except to ask her what her father's work was about.

"He has been working on a religious history of Britain," she answered.

"Ah, Early Christianity, Bede, that sort of thing," Harry commented politely. It sounded boring.

"No, although Father was preparing for ordination at one time. He is exploring the old religion."

"Old religion?"

"The practices of those who were responsible for the structures at Stonehenge and Avebury."

"Paganism?"

"Yes, one could call it that. But unfortunately that always carries a negative connotation. And the word itself originally only meant country dwellers. It is the connection to the earth that seems to distinguish our ancestors' belief from ours."

Harry stole a glance over at Miss Richmond. Yes, her silver-gilt hair was as glorious in the sun as he had imagined. Her profile would have delighted any artist. Yet here she was, picking her way along a path studded with sheep droppings, discoursing as though she were a don strolling the quad at Magdalene!

"And do you have a particular interest within this field?"

"Yes, I am trying to show that many of the customs that survive in our small villages today had their roots in ancient fertility rites."

Harry started coughing, and Lynette turned to him with immediate concern. "Oh, are we going too fast for you, Lord Sidmouth?"

"No, no, not at all. I'll be fine in a moment." *As soon as I can be sure I will not disgrace myself by laughing,* he thought. *What a wonderful irony: such a rare beauty and such frankness about matters, uh, physical,* he thought.

"Perhaps you will show me some of what you have been working on, Miss Richmond?"

Lynette looked over at him with such pleasure that Harry almost felt guilty. Almost. "I would be delighted to," she answered softly. "It is not often that anyone is interested. Or takes my interest seriously."

They had reached the main road into town by then, and as they joined the others, Harry felt that he was perhaps a little closer to his kiss than before they started.

Ten minutes later, as they walked up the High Street, Kate turned to the two men and pointed out the pub. "Our errands are rather commonplace," she announced. "The butcher, the baker—"

"The candlestickmaker," joked James. That was about as close to flirting as James would ever get, thought Harry with amusement. He wondered whether James was attracted to Miss Kate Richmond. They certainly seemed to have found enough to chat about during their walk.

"The greengrocers," said Kate with an appreciative smile. "Anyway, perhaps you would prefer a pint of ale, and we could arrange to meet you in an hour?"

Harry would have loved a pint, but was loathe to give up any time with Miss Richmond. He was pleased, therefore, when James immediately protested and said that they would be happy to accompany the two women on their errands.

And so they slowly proceeded up the street. They stopped at the butcher's to pick up bacon, and Kate explained that Lady Elizabeth said she put enough energy into her sheep, thank you, and would not raise her own pigs. They bought cheese. "This is our own Wensleydale," Kate told them proudly, as she broke off a few pieces and gave them to Harry and James, who were suitably impressed. "It has been made in the dale for centuries. In fact," she added, with a gleam in her eye, "we are also famous for our dairymaids. Or rather, I should say infamous. Centuries ago, the old abbots were so concerned about their morality, or lack thereof, that they restricted themselves to 'older, ill-favored' females!"

"Then certainly you and Miss Richmond would not have qualified," said James. "Not, that is to say," he continued, flustered by his foray into gallantry, "that you would be seeking employment as dairymaids. Or any sort of maid."

"Now, Jamie, you are only digging yourself deeper." Harry laughed. "Lord Clitheroe is not in the habit of complimenting young ladies," he explained.

"Lord Clitheroe," said Kate with a glint in her eye, "your compliments are gratefully accepted, all the more because they are sincere and unpracticed. A fresh compliment is worth so much more than old coin, don't you think, Lord Sidmouth?" she added with barbed sweetness.

"Absolutely, Miss Kate."

Harry had been watching Miss Richmond as James stumbled over his compliment. She neither blushed nor simpered, or indeed responded except to nod her agreement with her sister and give James a detached smile. She seemed to be removed from the whole conversation. Perhaps, thought Harry, she was thinking of fertility rites!

Their last stop was for the post. There were several letters, but one especially excited the Misses Richmond. It was on creamy, expensive-looking vellum and had already been franked.

"A letter from Gareth! From London. He and Arden must have already moved into Town for the Season. I am eager to get home now and hear the latest news."

As they made their way back, Harry found himself thinking about the remoteness of Richmond House. The two girls had grown up so differently from others of their class. A letter from London was probably a high point in their sheltered lives. That was what came of marrying for love, he thought. Lady Elizabeth an exile from her family. And her two daughters growing up in the wilds of Yorkshire. And yet they seemed a happy, if unconventional family.

The letter was placed on the parlor table where it would wait until teatime. The groceries were delivered to Janie, who, commenting on the lovely day, offered to make them a picnic.

"We *could* go partway up the fell," suggested Kate. "But perhaps you are not up to more walking, Lord Sidmouth."

Harry actually did not feel up to it. He would have been happier to take a nap. But he was not about to admit his weakness or give up any available time with the elusive Miss Richmond, so he just smiled and said a picnic sounded delightful.

"Are you sure, Harry?" asked James. "You do look a bit drawn."

"I am fine, James, I assure you," his friend answered

with the edge in his voice that meant: Don't press any further.

Janie prepared them a basket of cheese and apples and homemade bread. "I've put in cider for t' lasses and a few bottles of ale for t'gentlemen. Tha should enjoy tha lunch."

9

Kate, who had looked more closely at Lord Sidmouth as James questioned him, had seen the drawn look around his mouth. She was sure he was tired and just too stubborn to admit it. As she watched him walk ahead of her, she noticed that his limp was a bit more pronounced and that he was leaning heavily on his staff. And so she picked a spot closer to the house than she had originally planned, so that he did not have to do much climbing.

James spread out the rug, and Kate unwrapped the cheese and bread and placed them in the middle. "There. We shall be very informal and help ourselves."

There was only one knife, so Kate sliced the cheese and apples while the others pulled off chunks of bread.

"This may be the high point of our trip," said James contentedly, after a long swallow of ale.

"I would agree with you," Harry added. "The bluest sky, the best home brew, and most certainly, the natural beauty of Yorkshire." He turned to Lynette and gave her a slight bow.

Once again, her response was unexpected. She only smiled and gestured to the vista below them: green pastures divided neatly by stone walls spread out like a quilt. "It is a most beautiful place to live, isn't it?"

Let us see what the oh-so-charming Lord Sidmouth does with that, thought Kate, delighted at the look of chagrin that flitted across his face.

"I think that Lord Sidmouth was referring to a more particular beauty," said James with his eyes cast down, as though he was afraid to look up and see for himself Miss

Richmond's look of indifference. "You young ladies contribute to the specialness of the day."

Kate smiled and thanked him. Harry watched Lynette for her reaction. If his own practiced charm got nowhere, he assumed James's laborious compliments would also go unnoticed. He was surprised, therefore, to see Miss Richmond look quickly at James and than lower her own eyes, as though in embarrassment.

James, flustered by another unaccustomed foray into the world of flirtation, reached for his bottle of ale and took a long drink.

"How long have you lived in Sedbusk, Miss Kate?" asked Harry to break the rather charged silence.

"All my life, Lord Sidmouth. It was my father's inheritance, and when he and my mother eloped they came here."

Somehow it was hard for Harry to picture the slightly balding Mr. Richmond and the tall, spare Lady Elizabeth as ever being young and romantic enough to elope.

"The Tremayne family was against the match then?"

"Yes, my father came from a good family, but as a younger son, had nothing but this house to offer, once he decided not to continue in the church. Not that they would have been happy for my mother to marry a clergyman either."

"I would not have thought a life of scholarship lucrative enough to support a family. But I should not be so prying."

"That is all right, my lord. Your curiosity is understandable. My mother took over the sheep farm and made it a thriving business."

"Do you never feel lonely here?"

"Never. I cannot imagine a more beautiful place to live," said Kate. She was lying, of course, she thought to herself. Or at least, not telling the whole truth. It had been and was a wonderful place to live. But she was lonely, especially now that Gareth was gone. Oh, they had good neighbors and attended the occasional assembly in Bainbridge. But much as she loved her parents and her sister, she and Gareth were the only two in the family who were at all conscious of the unconventionality of their life. She was a practical young woman, she had no illusions, and she had realized a few years ago that she would probably never marry unless she ended up settling for one of the local gentlemen, most of whom were twenty years older. And she could not imagine Lynette finding someone sympathetic to her intellectual pursuits. Right this moment, looking up into Lord Sidmouth's very attractive face, she found herself minding her situation very much. Over the years she had met a few of Gareth's friends from university, but this was the first time she and her sister had socialized with two attractive and eligible men. It made her very conscious that what they were missing, most young girls of their class would have taken for granted.

Harry had at first taken her answer at face value, and then he noticed a swift change of expression on her face. He was willing to bet that Miss Kate Richmond, while appreciating the beauty of her surroundings, also missed the companionship of other young women and men. He felt a moment's sympathy for her, but then was drawn back into more general conversation with James.

After a few minutes the combination of ale and sun began to take effect, and Harry stretched himself out, head propped on his elbow. He gave up the attempt to keep up his part of the conversation, and very soon his eyes had closed as he dozed off.

It took a few minutes for the others to notice. It was only when James said, "Isn't that right, Harry?" and received no reply that the others realized what had happened.

"I apologize for Lord Sidmouth, ladies," said James. "I think the walking today did him in."

"We should get back to the house, but I hate to wake him," said Kate.

"Why don't I pack up and escort you and Miss Richmond back to the house," James suggested. "Then I will come back for Harry."

"Oh, I'd hate to have him awaken and think we had deserted him. Why don't I stay with him and we can return together."

"I am not sure I should leave you alone like that," James

responded hesitantly. "And shouldn't you accompany your sister?"

"I appreciate your concern, Lord Clitheroe," said Kate with a smile. "But we are less formal here in the country, and it is only a short way to the house, after all."

"Well, then, I will come back as quickly as I can."

Kate watched as James and Lynette made their way back down the path. He was very solicitous. No doubt both he and Lord Sidmouth had been captivated by Lynette's beauty. If her sister hadn't been so used to and indifferent to her effect on men, Kate might well have resented her. But as it was, she paid little attention to men's reactions.

Kate allowed herself to let go of all practical concerns and just sat there with her back against the stone wall, face up to the sun. She was not asleep, but so relaxed that she had almost forgotten her companion, when a nearby curlew's call must have awakened him.

He started up and looked around him wildly, as though the bird had been announcing danger. He appeared so distraught, that without thinking, Kate reached her hand out to his shoulder to reassure him. He instantly grabbed her wrist and pulling her down in front of him, he pinned her to the rug. When she let out a little cry of fear, he shook his head, his eyes focused, and he immediately released her. In the moment before he recognized her, Kate had seen on his face naked intent, as though for a second he was only all-focused will. She knew that had this been Spain, had she really been the enemy, she would have been dead within seconds.

She sat up and rubbed her wrist, watching him carefully for any sign of movement. He looked over, finally *seeing* her and realized her eyes were wide with fear. She looked like a deer caught in torchlight.

Harry ran both his hands through his hair, pulling at it as though to waken himself completely, and looked around as though to remind himself he was indeed in England and not on the Peninsula. Taking a deep breath, he let his hands drop to his knees, looking at them as if they were a stranger's.

"I am so sorry, Miss Richmond. I must have come out of a deep sleep very suddenly. I assure you, I am not in the habit of attacking women. In fact, I wasn't even aware at first that you were a woman."

"Oh, I could see that, my lord," whispered Kate.

Harry rubbed his hands over his eyes. "I must have frightened you terribly. I don't know what else to say except that when one is in the field, one survives only by developing the ability to react instantly, without thinking."

Kate just sat there, rubbing her wrist.

"Here, let me see your arm," Harry said, as gently as possible.

Kate held it out to him, looking as if she were afraid to refuse.

"You need not be afraid of me now, Miss Kate," he said. "I am very aware of where I am."

Her arm was red with the imprint of his fingers. "I am afraid you will have some bruises in the morning, but I don't think it is sprained," he said as he released it gently. "Where are James and your sister?"

"They returned to the house, my lord. We didn't want to disturb you, so I stayed here so that you wouldn't feel deserted when you awoke."

"And I repaid your act of kindness by hurting you."

"I am fine, my lord," answered Kate in a stronger voice. "And I think I understand."

"Do you, Miss Kate?" he said bitterly.

"I imagine it must be difficult to let go of all that enabled you to survive a war, my lord."

"Did your brother tell you anything of war, Miss Kate?"

"No, we never could get him to speak of it."

"Well, it is sometimes unspeakable."

They sat quietly for a moment, and then Kate said, "I think I see Lord Clitheroe coming up the path."

Harry got up, feeling stiff and old. When James reached them, Harry had already folded up the rug and handed it to his friend as James came up smiling and ready to tease Harry about his nap.

"I see you are awake at last!"

"Yes, James. Here, take the rug and Miss Kate and get them back to the house. I am going to take a few minutes to walk the stiffness out of my knee." Harry grabbed his staff and, turning his back on them both, limped up the path.

"Come, Lord Clitheroe, it is getting chillier and I would like to get back to the house. Lord Sidmouth needs some time on his own."

James saw that he would get no explanation of Harry's abrupt behavior from her, and so he offered his arm and they proceeded slowly down the path.

Although his knee was bothering him, Harry found the slow walk up the hill restored him to his surroundings. He was here, watching that stone, not there, a fine-tuned instrument of death. But he would not think of it, would not remember it. It was only in the in-between world of sleep that it came back to him. For the most part, if he kept himself busy, if he thought only of women and how he could get this one or that to kiss him, then he had no memories.

But how would he ever look Miss Kate Richmond in the face again?

10

It was close to teatime when Harry returned, and he changed quickly, wondering what, if anything, Miss Kate had told her sister or James. When he got to the table, however, he was greeted naturally by everyone, including Kate.

All the attention, he was relieved to discover, was focused on Lady Elizabeth, who was reading the letter they had picked up in Hawes. She was reading it to herself, with accompanying "hmms" and "aha's" when Kate finally let out her impatience.

"Mother! You are driving us all quite distracted. What does Gareth say?"

Her mother looked up and smiled. "Now Kate, you know that I don't read any letter aloud until I have read it myself first."

"Yes, but you are taking the longest time about it, Mother," complained Lynette.

James looked over at Harry and they both grinned. This was obviously a family ritual, and despite the complaints, they suspected the family enjoyed the familiar banter.

Finally Lady Elizabeth sighed, folded the letter, and placed it by her plate. "Well, my dears, I won't bore you by reading the whole thing. Much of what Gareth has written is about the lambing at Thorne, and how my advice on which ram to buy has proved fruitful, if you will forgive the pun."

"Mother, are you going to tell us what you were 'ahaing' about or not," Kate demanded.

Lady Elizabeth's eyes twinkled. "Your brother has invited you both for the Season. And I believe we should all go, don't you, Edward?"

Mr. Richmond, who had been drinking his tea and contemplating his latest chapter while the teasing had gone on, looked over at his wife. "Why, of course I agree, my dear."

"Edward, whatever will I do with you! Did you even hear what you are agreeing to?"

Mr. Richmond smiled across at his wife, and as she smiled back, Harry realized that for that short moment, no one else existed for either of them. The elopement story, which had seemed far too romantic for such a couple, now seemed not hard to believe, for the feeling of love and attraction between them was almost palpable. He wondered what it would be like, loving someone that long, despite receding hair, expanding waistlines, and wrinkles and gray hair.

"Well, what *did* I agree to, Elizabeth?" asked her husband.

"Gareth has invited the girls to London for the Season, and of course they must go."

"Of course. That is, if they wish to, my dear."

Harry had expected both young women to be in alt about the prospect of such an unexpected treat, but neither, to his surprise, was smiling. Both, in fact, looked like they were thinking over the offer very carefully.

"Well, Kate, Lynette, what do you think?" their father asked.

Lynette answered first. "I would love to see Gareth and Arden. And Aunt Kate. But we are right at a most important point in the book, Father."

"I too would love to make a family visit. But take part in the Season?" said Kate. "It seems overwhelming. We know no one and have nothing suitable to wear."

"Arden will sponsor you, my dears. You will have vouchers to Almacks, entree to the most important social occasions. You would enjoy yourselves immensely, I am sure," said her mother.

James cleared his throat. "You do know us, Miss Kate.

Lord Sidmouth and I will be the first to call and sign your dance cards, do you come," he said shyly.

Kate looked inquiringly over at Harry. "I am not so sure Lord Sidmouth would want to claim acquaintance with two such country mice as ourselves."

"You do me an injustice, Miss Kate. What better way could we show our gratitude for your hospitality."

"And you both do need the opportunity to meet suitable young gentlemen," added Mr. Richmond. "I am not so lost in my books as not to realize that," he said with a smile. "You cannot be editing and accounting forever, you know. You will want homes and families of your own."

Lynette frowned. "I have never even thought of getting married, Father. I am very happy staying here and helping you."

"But you must want a husband and children," said James without thinking. "Every woman does."

"But I don't," responded Lynette quite matter-of-factly.

Miss Lynette Richmond sat there looking like a painting by Sandro Botticelli while buttering her toast with ink-stained hands and declaring her intention to remain a spinster. Truly, thought Harry, of all the families they might have taken refuge with, the Richmonds had to be the most amusing. If only the two girls could be convinced, he would not have to worry about getting his kiss before he left. He would have all spring to work on the cool Miss Richmond and convince her that a husband might indeed be desirable. Not that he wanted to be that husband, of course. But he would like to be the one to warm her up for whomever it was.

While Harry was amused and challenged by Lynette's pronouncement, James sat there torn between anticipation and despair. Miss Lynette Richmond had captured his interest as no other woman had ever been able to do. He had been dreading the fact that they would have to leave, and he would have no excuse to see her again. And now here was this wonderful opportunity—and her reaction. Unlike Harry, he knew she meant it. She had not responded to either Harry's expert address nor his own clumsy attempts at compliments. She seemed genuinely uninterested in leaving Yorkshire. And even if she did come to Town for the Season, how would he ever get beyond her indifference?

"Neither your mother nor I would ever force you into marriage, my dear," her father reassured her. "But going to London would mean being able to use the resources of the British Museum. And," he continued thoughtfully, "you know how much I have wanted to visit Cornwall in the spring. London is that much closer to the southwest," he mused.

Lynette's face lit up. "Why that is true, Father. I had not thought of it."

Kate smiled at her sister's sudden enthusiasm. "Well, I suppose it is not such a bad idea," she said. "And if we hate it, we will all go haring off to Cornwall mid-Season."

"Are you as disinterested in marriage as your sister?" Harry asked her.

"That is a rather impertinent inquiry, Lord Sidmouth," Kate answered tartly. "But then, we have been treating you quite informally, and letting you know our family business, so I suppose I must forgive you."

"But not answer me?"

"I will answer after you, my lord. Do you want a wife and children?"

"Touché, Miss Kate. Yes, I know what I owe to my name and title. I do plan to marry."

"That is not exactly what I asked, but I will accept your answer, my lord."

"And give me yours?" prodded Harry.

"I would like to marry and have children. But I would also be content to remain with my family," she added, with a glint in her eye.

Lady Elizabeth had been listening to their exchange with hidden amusement. "It seems we are all in agreement. This Season will see the Richmond family in London," she announced.

11

Later that evening, Lynette sat in front of her mirror, watching her hair grow brighter as she brushed it down over her shoulders. She knew she was beautiful. How could she not, when she had the evidence in front of her every day, and when everyone had been telling her so for years.

What no one seemed to understand, however, was how vulnerable it made her feel. She had no control over the attention she attracted, and this attention had nothing to do with the real Lynette. It had only to do with an accident of birth. Sometimes she felt more like a young girl than a beautiful woman, and the only way to keep that young girl safe was to use remoteness as a shield.

It was one thing, moreover, to experience that vulnerability in the small, local assemblies. It would be quite another to subject herself to a Season in London. There she would be dealing with sophisticated gentlemen like Harry Lifton and James Otley. Although sophisticated was not quite the word to describe Lord Clitheroe, she thought, smiling to herself. She found his awkward compliments rather endearing. Lord Sidmouth's attentions, on the other hand, felt a little frightening.

She had spoken sincerely at the supper table: she had never dreamed of marriage and children. She had thrown all her energy into her scholarly work and was not at all disturbed by the prospect of living her life as a bluestocking spinster aunt, enjoying her brother's and sister's children. But Kate was as unlikely to marry as she unless they went to London, and she could not hold her sister back from wider opportunities, if she indeed wanted them.

* * *

Kate, who was getting herself ready for bed, heard a soft knock at her door.

"Come in."

Lynette opened the door and came over and perched at the end of Kate's bed. Kate patted the space next to her. "Come under the covers, Lynnie. It is too cold to sit there."

Lynette smiled at the old childhood name and climbed in next to her sister. "What do you think of going to London, Kate?"

"I think it is frightening, exciting, and about time the Richmonds returned to the world."

"And are you so eager then to leave home and get married?"

"I do wish for a family of my own," said Kate. "And I do not want to settle for one of our neighbors."

"Why, you are not drawn to Mr. Heathcote?" teased Lynette, and they both giggled, for the aforesaid Mr. Heathcote was a widower with six children. He came visiting frequently with the obvious intention of persuading one of the Richmond sisters to become his second wife.

"And are you truly as uninterested, Lynnie, as you claim to be? Do you want children?"

"It is not so much that I am against marriage, Kate, as I see no particular reason to be for it. I am very happy with my life. And what man wants a bluestocking for a wife?"

"If she were as beautiful as you are, I would think quite a few."

"My beauty isn't me, Kate. Sometimes it feels like a thing outside myself, keeping me separate from the rest of the world. The real me is the person who loves research and writing. When I look in a mirror . . . well, I admit, I can understand what people admire. But sometimes that gilt-haired woman feels like a stranger."

Kate knew her sister spoke the truth. She herself was much more at home in her body. She loved to walk and ride and dance. She also loved to read, and truly enjoyed working with numbers, but the obsessiveness with which Lynette sought her books was foreign to her. And when she looked in the mirror, she saw herself, Kate Richmond, who was very comfortable with her curly brown hair and gray eyes.

"And what do you think of Lords Sidmouth and Clitheroe?" asked Kate, changing the subject.

Lynette paused for a minute. "I think I am a little frightened of Lord Sidmouth."

"Why? What has he done?" demanded her sister.

Lynette looked at Kate with surprise. "Why, nothing. It is just a feeling I have when he focuses his attention on me. But he has been a perfect gentleman, Kate," she said, surprised at her sister's outburst.

"Humph. I don't trust that perfect gentleman," she said. "But what of Lord Clitheroe?" Kate was most interested in the answer, for she had noticed Clitheroe's attempts at compliments and thought him just the sort of gentleman her sister needed.

"I like him, for he seems quite a kind man," answered Lynette. "They are very different, aren't they? How odd that they are such good friends."

Lynette's tone and expression had revealed nothing. It seemed she had not responded to Lord Clitheroe's interest. And Kate was sometimes as puzzled by her sister's indifference as were James and Harry. Lynette, who appeared fragile and angelically beautiful, seemed to keep herself behind an invisible barrier. And Kate was not sure that anyone would ever get beyond it.

"Yes, they are an odd pair," said Kate. "I am grateful for that snowstorm, though, for it will be reassuring to recognize at least two faces in Town."

James and Harry stayed three more days. Harry was up and out on the fells early, once with James and twice alone. But before they left, they made sure to walk up to Gabriel's hut and thank him and Benjamin once again.

"Tha looks a different person, lad," said the old shepherd to Harry. "Tha knee isn't holding tha back?"

"No, I think I am completely recovered. We were very lucky to have been taken in by you and the Richmonds."

"Yes," said James. "They have been wonderful to us."

"Oh, aye. They are good folk and good neighbors."

The men chatted awhile about the weather, which was growing consistently warmer, and the intelligence of sheep-dogs, as they watched Benjamin gather a few ewes and their lambs together so that Gabriel could bring them up to higher pasture. Gabriel only had to signal by a whistle or a hand motion and the dog knew exactly what to do.

"He is an amazing animal," exclaimed James.

"Aye, he is a good lad."

"We will not forget either of you," said Harry, offering Gabriel his hand.

"Coom back again, lads. The dales are beautiful in t'fall."

"Perhaps we will, Gabriel."

"Do you mean that, Harry?" asked James as they walked down the path to the house.

"There is something about this countryside, James. I wouldn't mind coming back to finish our walk."

"Nor I."

The two men left the next morning, having decided to hire a chaise to York, where Harry's coach would meet them. They said their good-byes and thank yous at the breakfast table, but before the chaise drove up, Harry sought Kate out in the office, where she was going over the accounts.

"Miss Kate?"

"Oh, you are still here, my lord," she said, looking up in surprise.

"So eager to have me gone?" he teased.

"Now, you know I didn't mean it that way."

"You would have some reason for it," continued Harry seriously. "I came to see if you had forgiven me for the incident the other day. We have both pretended it did not happen, but I would not like to leave, or indeed, meet you in London, knowing you were angry with me still."

"I assure you, I was more frightened than angry, Lord

Sidmouth. And there is nothing to forgive. You were not intending to hurt me."

"Thank you for being so understanding. I hope you will save me a waltz when we meet in London."

"I doubt I will have to save you anything, my lord. I don't expect our cards to be full."

"Oh, I would not be so sure of that, Miss Kate. I suspect you and your sister will be pleasantly surprised."

"Thank you for your reassurance. I confess I need all the encouragement I can get."

"Until London, then." Kate stood up and offered her hand. Harry shook it and then turned it over, inspecting her fingers. "One thing I would recommend for both the Richmond sisters is a good scrubbing before your first ball," he said, pointing to the inkstains.

Kate laughed. "I will be sure we follow your suggestion, Lord Sidmouth. Good-bye, and have a pleasant journey."

12

The Richmonds left a week later in Gareth's traveling coach which he had sent up to them. They arrived at his town house late in the afternoon and were shown immediately to their rooms to rest from their long journey. They had been informed by the butler that the marquess and his lady were out, but expected back for dinner, and that the dowager was napping.

Although her mother and sister settled in for a nap before dinner, Kate was too restless after hours in the coach to lie down. She had not been to London for many years, and she was curious to see how much had changed in the Thorne town house.

It was clear from her little tour that her sister-in-law was not interested in radically altering the decor. Some rooms had obviously been refurbished and a few newly decorated, but nothing was a radical departure from what Kate remembered. All in all, Kate was pleased with both Arden's taste and sensitivity.

She had just decided to settle herself in the library when she heard someone coming down the stairs.

"Aunt Kate! It is so wonderful to see you," she exclaimed when she saw it was the dowager marchioness.

"My dear Kate," said the small gray-haired lady, holding out her hands. "I am so glad Gareth and Arden convinced you all to come. Here, let me ring for some sherry, and we will have a nice private coze before anyone else comes down."

They seated themselves in the drawing room and sipped

their sherry and nibbled sweet wafers while Kate entertained her aunt with amusing tales from their journey.

"But I am not at all altogether sure we should have come," she concluded.

"Whyever not?"

"We know so few people. And we are neither heiresses nor sweet, young seventeen-year-olds. Just—"

"—two daughters of an unconventional couple who are also cursed with an eccentric aunt dubbed the Methodist Marchioness?"' suggested the dowager, with a twinkle in her eye.

"Well, since you have said it, I can only agree." Kate laughed. "You must admit there is nothing to particularly recommend us."

"There is your charm and wit and intelligence. And your attractiveness and Lynette's great beauty. And, of course, you will have your brother and sister-in-law's sponsorship."

"Is that an advantage or a disadvantage?" asked Kate, only half-teasing. "After all, Arden was known as the Insufferable."

"Oh, she has lived down her reputation these last two years. There are some who still don't like her outspokenness, but she has made quite a few friends. And her cousin married Lord Heronwood. That will get you entry everywhere."

"Actually, we *do* have two acquaintances, Aunt Kate, who have promised us each a waltz."

"And who might they be?"

"Lords Clitheroe and Sidmouth."

"However did you meet our David and Jonathan?"

"They are devoted friends, aren't they?"

"Yes, and because they are so different, they are often teased about it. But however did you come across them?"

"They were on a walking tour in Yorkshire and were caught in one of our sudden spring storms near Sedbusk. They were our guests for several days."

"I am glad to hear that Harry Lifton is well enough to be going on a walking trip. He came home in dreadful shape."

"Aside from a slight cough and a weak knee, he seems recovered."

"And how did you like the two gentlemen?"

"I found Lord Clitheroe most likable: kind and thoughtful. He was quite taken with Lynette."

"And what of Sidmouth?"

"He was also taken with Lynette, Aunt Kate. He seems much more experienced with the ladies, judging by the ease of his address and his rather practiced charm." Kate's tone clearly indicated that she didn't quite approve of such expertise.

"He always was a charmer," agreed her aunt. "Took after his father, the late marquess. And he also inherited his mother's Welsh intensity—a powerful combination. I knew his parents, you know. She was a few years younger than I, but the marquess was one of my own admirers my first Season. Of course, once Maria was out, he had eyes for no one else. Which, given the fact he had his eye on every pretty woman, from young miss to widow . . . ! But he was never quite as shameless in his behavior as Harry was this past Little Season. He has become something more than charming. He is a bit more of a rake, in fact, than his father ever was—quite careless of the feelings of susceptible young women. What was Lynette's reaction to him? I would not want to see her hurt."

"You know Lynnie, Aunt Kate. She is oblivious to all the attention she draws. I had hoped she would respond to Lord Clitheroe. I think he is just the sort of man she needs: steady and attentive and trustworthy."

"Oh, yes, the Clitheroes have always been known for their solidity and devotion to duty. There is a bishop in the family, you know. I wonder what they would think of a connection with the Richmonds or Tremaynes?"

"Now, what aspersions are you casting on our families, Aunt Kate?" said a deep voice from the door.

"Gareth!" Kate jumped up and hurled herself into her brother's arms. "Oh, it is *so* good to see you."

Gareth smiled down at his favorite sister. "It is delightful that you are here. I am glad Father suggested it."

"Father suggested this!"

"Yes, dear little sister. It was Father's idea that Arden sponsor your come-out. He is not that lost to the realities of the everyday world, you know."

"But we would have suggested it ourselves, had he not done so," said a voice behind Gareth. "Welcome to London, Kate."

Kate stepped back from her brother and smiled at her sister-in-law, who had just stepped in behind him. Arden looked stunning in a dark blue walking dress that matched her eyes and complimented her black hair and fair complexion. Gareth reached back and, putting his arm around his wife, pulled her forward. "We are both looking forward to seeing you and Lynette taking the Town by storm."

"Well, save tha breath to cool tha porridge," said Kate in broad Yorkshire. "Lynnie will likely create a sensation, but we are hardly material to become reigning toasts."

Gareth looked at his sister with mock despair. "So little faith in your brother's influence?"

"No, rather a realistic assessment of the Richmond family."

Gareth laughed, as they all did, but with all his appreciation of Kate's humorous summary of their family's reputation, he was a bit worried about her. She was his favorite sister, the one he felt closest to. Oh, he loved Lynnie, who could not? But he and Kate were the practical ones, the objective Richmonds, the two who took charge. And his absence these past few years, both in the military and now at Thorne, meant that Kate had had to take on even more responsibility. He was determined to see that her Season was a success and that she was not overshadowed by her beautiful older sister.

13

For the next two weeks Arden, Kate, and Lynette spent much of their time shopping. At first Kate protested the extravagant sums Arden seemed determined to spend, but she was assured that Gareth could well afford it and that he wanted to spare no expense. Kate finally let herself begin to enjoy it. She had very little luxury in her life and few clothes that weren't practical. To be offered such a choice of color and fabric overwhelmed her at first, but soon she became quite good at determining what flattered her and what complimented Lynette's beauty.

Lynette offered no protests, but neither did she involve herself. She usually brought a book with her to keep occupied while Kate was being fitted. When it was her turn, she stood patiently and obeyed the dressmaker's commands to lift her arm or make a quarter turn. Occasionally a particularly beautiful silk caught her attention, but for the most part, she might well have still been holding her book in front of her nose.

"Has Lynette always been like this?" Arden asked her husband after one particularly frustrating day.

"Like what?" asked Gareth.

"She so often seems like she is living in another world—one where perfectly fitting clothes magically appear in one's wardrobe. Does she really wish for this Season, Gareth?"

"Lynette has always been, well . . . Lynette. She is more like Father than Kate or I," Gareth admitted.

"But your father, as distracted as he can become by his work, seems more anchored in the real world. When he is with your mother, for instance, he is well aware of his surroundings. Lynette isn't just absentminded, or always with her head in a book. Well, she *is* always with a head in her book! But it goes beyond that. It is as though all her energy is locked away inside."

"I hadn't really thought of it that way before," admitted Gareth. "I've always loved and accepted Lynette for who she is—an unusually beautiful, intelligent, but absentminded young woman. Maybe we have all taken that too much for granted."

"She is gloriously beautiful, Gareth. So breathtaking that one cannot even be envious. One feels it is a privilege to see her, like looking at a painting come to life. But that is just it. She hides herself so well behind that beauty."

"She won't be able to do that as easily in London as in Sedbusk. In fact, this Season may be just what she needs to take her out of herself."

Lady Thorne was not the only one who was concerned about Lynette. The dowager marchioness, who had visited Richmond House regularly, had known, of course, how different the two girls were, but not until they arrived did she feel that she appreciated the extent of the difference. And she worried about them both.

Kate was of such a practical nature and so used to taking charge, that her aunt wondered if she ever indulged herself in the romantic daydreams the way young ladies did. She seemed to be enjoying herself and excited about her new clothes and excursions to the historic sights of London. But she didn't seem to have much hope of forming an attachment or even making a suitable, practical match. She seemed perfectly willing to look upon the Season as an enjoyable interlude and then return to her parents' home.

And Lynette was even more worrisome. She was certainly a daydreamer, but not, the dowager was convinced, of handsome young men. No, she was entirely concentrated upon her father's book and her research for it. And the only time she became animated was when her aunt questioned her about their progress.

The subject matter of their research, investigating stone and chalk carvings and traditional celebrations to determine their connection to fertility rituals, was hardly one a gently born young lady should be conversant with. It was one thing for the marchioness to have made her charitable activity distributing hygienic information to women of the streets. She was a married woman, now widowed, of a certain age. It was quite another for an innocent young woman like Lynette to go on about the number of church carvings of women displaying their private parts and what that might say about the influence of the early religions upon Christianity! Lynette discussed her research in such a detached and scholarly manner that there was no difference in her tone when she talked about the foliated heads of the Green Man carvings and those of the female exhibitionists!

Her familiarity with such subject matter a stranger might have attributed to her experience in romantic matters. The dowager knew that nothing could be further from the truth. Lynette's very matter-of-factness and her ignorance of the incongruity of such interest being expressed by such a beautiful young lady, told her aunt that her niece was emotionally and romantically quite ignorant.

And that was what worried her. Not that a young woman should expertly discuss fertility rituals, but that her niece had no interest in forming an everyday relationship with a young man. Some part of Lynette seemed asleep and inaccessible, and her aunt wondered whether a prince's kiss could wake her up.

14

After his sisters had completed their new wardrobes, Gareth decided it was time for them to be seen by Society. One late afternoon he arranged for the landau to be brought round and they set out for the park. It had been a warm, sunny day, and both young women were dressed in white muslin gowns trimmed in different colors, Kate's in Nile green and Lynette's with blue ribbons that matched her eyes. As they entered the park, the sun was low in the sky, and Gareth noticed how the late afternoon light lit the red highlights in Kate's hair and made Lynette's look like spun silver. He smiled to himself, thinking that it shouldn't take but a few minutes for the young men to notice them and he was right. Mere acquaintances were bowing and lifting their hats and would have surrounded the carriage had Gareth allowed it. He proceeded on, however, wanting only to pique an interest in his sisters. But when Lords Clitheroe and Sidmouth approached on horseback, there was no choice. He had to stop and let them greet their former hostesses.

James dismounted and immediately came up to Lynette, who smiled and calmly stated that she was happy to see him again. It was hardly an effusive greeting, but James didn't care. He was too bemused by Lynette's beauty to notice anything lacking.

Lord Sidmouth had bowed to the ladies, but was busy renewing his acquaintance with Gareth.

"I did not immediately connect Captain Richmond with the Marquess of Thorne. It was quite a surprise to me," he said.

"My uncle had no relations on his side and so he arranged for me to be his legal heir. But it was not a fact generally known, and never spoken of even in the family very much. I left Portugal to be with him when he was dying and to support my aunt."

"You were well out of it," said Harry.

"I hear Badajoz was a bloodbath."

"Yes."

The two men looked at one another, and Kate, who was on that side of the carriage and had been listening in on their conversation, thought that a world of experience foreign to her had been conveyed in that terse interchange.

"I see you are looking fully recovered, Lord Sidmouth," she observed, breaking the silence.

He smiled at her, then turned to Gareth and said: "James and I owe your family our lives."

"You owe Gabriel and Benjamin your lives. We only took you in after your rescue," Kate answered lightly.

"The Richmond hospitality will not easily be forgotten. But excuse me. I must say hello to Miss Richmond." Harry handed his reins to Gareth, who took them without thinking, and then looked down at his hands as if to say, now how did he manage that? Meanwhile, Lord Sidmouth crossed in front of the carriage and made his way to Lynette's side, where he flashed his most charming smile and gave her an extravagant compliment.

Gareth looked quizzically at Kate and they both grinned. "You don't mind, Kate?" he asked in a low voice. "I am afraid that initially at least, Lynette will draw them like bees to flowers."

"I have had years to get used to it, Gareth."

"But London is different from Yorkshire, my dear."

"Ah, but Lynette is the same, Gareth."

"Well, that is true." And they both smiled at each other again, remembering all the young men who initially flocked to their sister at local assemblies, then fell away gradually as the compliments and flirting seemed to fall on deaf ears. Quite often Lynette, who had been the center of attention at the beginning of an evening, by the end would be holding up the wall. And Kate, who had been overshadowed at first, would have danced almost every dance.

James, who had been edged out by Harry, came around to pay his compliments to Kate. While the three of them chatted amiably, Kate kept her eye on Lord Sidmouth and her sister. He was obviously a practiced charmer, and he seemed to be eliciting a little more of a response from Lynette than most young men did. Not that she was simpering or blushing, but she was conversing with more animation than usual about the weather, the sights and scenes of London, and the upcoming Peverell ball.

Before Lord Sidmouth's attention could become too marked, Gareth announced that it was time to move on. The men remounted, and all agreed they were looking forward to their meeting at the Peverells'.

As they rode away, James realized he was furious with Harry. Since this had never happened before, he hardly knew what to say. Surely Harry had noticed his interest in Miss Richmond? Why, then, did he seem intent on making her his next flirt? He would be damned if he would allow Harry to gain her affection and then toss it away as he had with the others in the fall. Despite her calm exterior and seeming untouchability, James sensed that Miss Richmond was vulnerable. And how could she not eventually respond to Harry's expert charm?

Harry had of course noticed James's infatuation. It would have been hard to miss it. But he thought it was only that, an infatuation with Lynette's striking appearance. She was not at all the sort for his staid friend. James needed someone more forceful, like her sister Kate. His friend might be a little piqued by Harry's conquest, and he had never before done anything to hurt him. But some imp of perversity seemed to have a hold on him. He was as driven as he had been in the fall when he first returned to Town. Some sort of hard energy had taken him over, an energy that could not or would not let up. And he had to let himself flow with it, regardless of friendship or the feelings of vulnerable young women. If he didn't, he knew he would be back in Hell.

15

On the evening of the ball, Arden had decided that an informal, intimate family supper would be preferable to accepting one of their many invitations to dine out. That way they would arrive later in the evening, missing the inevitable crush, and she hoped, relaxed by the informality.

Accordingly they arrived at the Peverells' a good half hour after most of the guests. Lady Peverell greeted them warmly, but waved them into the ballroom where Arden was greatly relieved to see her Aunt Ellen, her cousin Celia, and Celia's husband, Lord Heronwood.

"Come, let me introduce you to my family," she said and led them all over.

Both her aunt and cousin were delighted to make the Richmonds' acquaintance.

"We just arrived in Town yesterday," explained Arden's aunt. "I am so sorry we could not have been here to welcome you, but Celia is a most unfashionable and indulgent mother and hated to drag her son away from the country where he enjoys both his parents' constant attention."

"Have you been enjoying London, Kate?" Heronwood asked.

Kate smiled and chatted away about their visits to the Tower and Astley's, all the while thinking that she must be very wicked, but the only thing she could think of as they talked was the amazing aptness of Heronwood's name. Gareth had of course told her how Arden had earned her title of "Insufferable," and she had had great sympathy for the victims of her wit. But she had to admit to herself that the temptation in this case would have been great, for Lord

Heronwood, with his height, long nose, and weak chin, re-sembled nothing so much as a marsh bird.

The ballroom was ablaze with candles, and Lynette was standing by a pillar set with a large candelabra. When the present country dance ended and the couples began to leave the floor, the dancers were struck by the vision of a young woman in ivory silk, her hair scintillating in the candle-light. Within moments a crowd had formed around the Richmonds, with young men begging for introductions.

James, who had been making his way slowly toward the family, watched with disappointment as he saw the tri-umphant young Hornden lead Miss Richmond off for the next country dance. Kate had received a rather backhanded invitation from one of the disappointed pursuers, and the rest of the family was keeping Arden's aunt, Mrs. Denbigh, company. When James joined them, he gallantly asked Mrs. Denbigh for her hand in the next dance and received warm smiles from her and her daughter.

When the next dance turned out to be a waltz, he was therefore already committed and had to watch Harry, who had appeared out of nowhere, capture Miss Richmond and lead her back to the dance floor.

Harry had planned his strategy carefully. He had no de-sire for a country dance. He wanted to hold Miss Richmond a little bit closer for much longer. As they moved out onto the dance floor, he complimented Lynette on her dress, a compliment she accepted calmly and matter-of-factly, as usual. She was a graceful dancer, he discovered, and they were a well-matched couple. Arden remarked to Gareth as she watched them glide by, that Lynette resembled a faerie queen and Lord Sidmouth one of her knights. "Perhaps be-cause he is part Welsh," said Gareth. "He does have a fey air about him."

Harry himself was both appreciating Lynette's other-worldly beauty and wondering if he could ever pierce her reserve, which was as great as if she had been a member of the royal family. She answered his questions about her time in London; she smiled automatically at one of his jokes.

She let him pull her in a bit closer, but there was no flush of embarrassment as he squeezed her waist and pulled her hand in to rest on his shoulder for a moment. Any other young woman would have been blushing and stammering with nerves, or letting herself brush up against him. Not Miss Richmond. It was as though she were immune to his formidable charm, and that only made him want her the more.

When the waltz ended, Harry asked if he could bring her something from the refreshment table. Her face opened up for a moment with gratitude. "Thank you, my lord. It is hot in here and I am quite thirsty."

James, however, was ahead of him. James, who had been watching them as he whirled Mrs. Denbigh around the dance floor, who had felt his temperature rise at the sight of Harry pulling Lynette in close, was determined not to leave them alone. And so he had led Mrs. Denbigh over to where Lynette waited and was chatting with both of them when Harry returned with his two glasses of punch.

Lynette smiled her gratitude, and Harry offered his glass to Arden's aunt.

"Harry, be a good fellow and get me a glass when you go back for your own," asked James, who was amazed at his own temerity. "I don't want to leave the ladies alone."

"Of course, James," replied Harry, amused at his friend's obvious tactics, and went off again. He was no more than amused, for he knew that ultimately James didn't stand a chance.

When he returned, Lord and Lady Heronwood had joined the group, and Harry let the conversation rise and fall around him as he stood quietly drinking in Miss Richmond's beauty. The same associations with the old ballads came to his mind as they had to Arden's. Would it be as dangerous to court Miss Richmond, wondered Harry, as it was for Thomas the Rhymer and Tam Lin to be lovers of the faerie queen? And what was it about Miss Richmond, aside from her beauty, that made her so irresistible, that made her, for the time being at least, the only woman who could hold his attention?

He invited Lady Heronwood to dance, and then Lady Arden, but he had no desire to lead any other young lady out onto the floor. All his energy was concentrated on one exquisitely beautiful young woman.

16

Kate, to her great relief, had not been lacking in dance partners. No crowd of eager young men ebbed and flowed around her as around her sister, but her dance card was almost full. No one stood out for her, but on the other hand, no one who asked her to dance was twenty years older and looking for a mother for his children, which in itself was an improvement over the Yorkshire assemblies! A few of the young men made it obvious by their questions that they had only asked her to dance to get closer to her sister. But most seemed genuinely interested in her, and one or two signed themselves for a second dance.

Lord Clitheroe was one of her more enjoyable partners. Although she had watched his attempts to converse with Lynette and his one dance with her, he did not let his preoccupation with one sister make him impolite to the other. He was genuinely interested in Kate's reactions to the ball, and she felt quite at ease with him as well as sympathetic. It annoyed her to see how Lord Sidmouth pursued her sister, for he must know of his best friend's interest. She was determined to see if she could in any way help Lord Clitheroe, and when their dance ended, she smiled brightly up at him and asked him to walk her over to where Lynette and Harry were chatting with Gareth and Arden.

When the next waltz was struck, Kate quickly flashed her dance card at the marquess and said brightly: "I believe this dance is ours, Lord Sidmouth?" As a matter of fact, he had not signed for it at all, but as a gentleman, could hardly deny her, and they moved off, leaving James with Lynette.

"This is one of my very few dances with my wife. Will you partner Lynette, Lord Clitheroe?" Gareth requested.

James flushed, and Lynette, noticing his embarrassment, reassured him.

"You do not need to, my lord. I am quite content to watch."

"No, no. I would be delighted to lead you out, Miss Richmond."

James might have been less adept with light conversation and banter than Harry, but he was as good a dancer, and once they had been on the floor for a few measures, he felt more sure of himself. His arm tightened around Lynette's waist, and they swept gracefully around the dance floor.

"There is something very solidly human about our faerie queen's present partner," commented Arden to her husband as they waltzed by.

"Most certainly Clitheroe is no elfin knight."

"I think your sister needs someone more earth-bound, Gareth. A queen, faerie or otherwise, can lead a very lonely life."

"Do you think Lynnie is lonely, Arden? She always seems quite content within herself."

"There is something in Lynette that reminds me of myself."

"No two women could be more different," protested Gareth.

"In many ways, yes. But she is as remote from human warmth in her own way as I was in mine. She may not need a Captain Rudesby, as I did, to bring her down to earth, but I think Lord Clitheroe might do very well for her."

Gareth smiled at his wife. "I am glad your tongue has a few barbs left, My Lady Thorne, or else I would wonder whom I married." Gareth pulled his wife closer to him and murmured in her ear that he was very eager to see this evening end, before he released her back into a more respectable position.

Harry had been more amused than annoyed at Kate's manipulation. He was not worried about losing a dance to

James for he knew, in the end, he was much more likely to win the lady. Or at least her heart. He had no real desire for her hand, he reminded himself.

He looked down at Kate and smiled. "I do not believe I recall signing your dance card, Miss Richmond."

Kate decided to abandon all pretense, now that she had achieved her goal. "You didn't," she snapped. "But Lord Clitheroe needed some help, and I decided to give it to him. He is your best friend. Aren't you ashamed to be in competition with him?"

"All's fair in love and war, Miss Kate," responded Harry lightly, refusing to be drawn into a quarrel.

"If all you can do is justify your behavior with clichés, then you are even more hopeless than I thought."

Harry opened his mouth to say something in his own defense and then closed it again, and his arm convulsively tightened around Kate's fingers, squeezing them painfully. All of a sudden he could hear his words given back to him in cockney accents, in the town of Badajoz. "All's fair hin love and war, Captin," the solider had said with a wink and knowing smile, as if Harry would understand and overlook his actions.

Kate's exclamation of pain brought his mind back to the dance floor. When he realized what he had done, he loosened his grip and apologized. "I beg your pardon, Miss Kate. I was . . . somewhere else for the moment."

Kate looked up, wondering if this incident was similar to what happened on their picnic, but the marquess's eyes told her nothing. He said nothing for the rest of their dance, but held her so lightly they were barely connected. When the dance ended he led her across the dance floor to Gareth and Arden. Just before they reached them, he turned to her and said, "James is only infatuated with your sister, Miss Kate. It will do him no real harm to be cut out."

He had hoped this explanation would soften her antagonism toward him and was taken aback when she rounded on him and said softly but with suppressed anger, "And are you God, Lord Sidmouth, to know the exact state of your friend's heart? But at least he has one to be injured. You, I fear, do not, and nothing to give my sister but empty charm. Thank you for the dance," she concluded, biting the words out.

Harry bowed to her back as she walked away from him. Perhaps she was right. Perhaps he had no heart. But if having one meant believing, as he used to, in love and honor and the ultimate goodness of human beings, then after what he had seen at Badajoz, he no longer wanted one.

17

Over the next few weeks the pattern that had been set at the Peverell ball continued. Both James and Harry paid their attentions to Lynette. Their rivalry remained unacknowledged, however, for James was not about to lose any dignity by revealing the state of his heart, and Harry still did not see his friend as a serious threat.

Kate had gathered a small circle of admirers. She showed no preferences for any of them, but bestowed her favors equally and found herself enjoying her Season more than she would have expected. Lynette so far had no occasion to hold forth at length on her scholarly interests, and therefore no opportunity to offend anyone's sensibilities. She accepted Clitheroe's and Sidmouth's invitations equally, having told Kate early on that since she had no particular interest in either, she had no intention of favoring one over the other and ruining an old friendship. Kate suspected that despite her sister's care, the friendship had been changed forever.

She was right. James and Harry had known each other since Eton where James had taken on a protective role almost immediately. James had been taller and stronger and had been at school a year when Harry arrived in the middle of a term. As a new boy, he was, of course, a target, and one day James had rescued him from a group of older boys who were teasing him about being Welsh. Harry had taken them all on and, when James arrived on the scene, was being held down on the ground by one of them and pummeled by the others. James waded right in, scattering the tormentors, although not before taking a few blows himself. Their "war wounds," a black eye and bloody nose apiece, brought them together. The differences in temperament worked for their friendship, rather than against it, for James's seriousness and slow steady way of working complemented Harry's quicksilver personality. They were inseparable from then on, visiting each other's homes during the holidays and continuing on to Oxford together.

All through the years James had been the steadying influence. Although there were times when he felt dull compared to his friend, for the most part he knew that he was also, in some ways, stronger than Harry. When they first came down from college, he guided Harry away from the wilder set of young men and kept him from excesses in drinking and gambling. At the same time, he enjoyed Harry's more "conservative" friends, for their energy and humor kept him from becoming too serious.

Although there was only six months' difference between them, James had always felt like a protective older brother, and never more so than when Harry went off to war and returned seriously wounded. But that had all changed. The war had affected Harry not just in the obvious physical ways, although James could not quite put his finger on how. James had begun to feel more protective of the young ladies Harry was setting out to charm than of his friend himself. And none had raised his protective instincts more than Miss Lynette Richmond.

At first he had been drawn only to her beauty. But the more time he spent with her, the more he sensed a vulnerability under her absentminded air and the more he wanted to get to know the real Miss Richmond. And while he was not at all sure she would consider him as a suitor, he was absolutely certain that Harry could never make her happy. Harry was playing the same game he had in the fall, although more intently and exclusively, but James knew his heart was not involved. And, if he were wrong, then this time Harry would just have to take care of himself.

As the unspoken rivalry continued, Kate wondered whether Lynette had formed a preference. She never by a blush or stammer revealed any deeper feeling for either of them. One evening, after they had returned from a dinner dance, Kate decided to ask her if her response had at all changed.

She knocked gently at her sister's door and whispered, "Are you still awake, Lynnie?"

"Come in, Kate."

Kate slipped in and perched on the edge of the bed, watching her sister brush her hair out.

"However do you balance your attention to Lord Clitheroe and Lord Sidmouth, Lynnie? I was watching you tonight and wondering if you keep a running tally on the sticks of your fan!"

Her sister turned and looked at her inquiringly. "Don't you think it important for me not to get in the way of a long and close relationship, Kate? I have been trying very hard to show no preference, as you know."

"I am only teasing you," Kate apologized. "It is just that it is hard to imagine that you have no real preference, however you may conceal it. Do you like one over the other?"

"I enjoy Lord Sidmouth's sense of humor, and he is a good dancer. But I feel much more comfortable with Lord Clitheroe. I think he wishes to know the real me, whereas Lord Sidmouth is only in pursuit of my beauty. And he is still a bit frightening to me," she added thoughtfully. "Oh, he has never been anything other than a gentleman," she said as Kate began to sputter. "It is just that I can feel he has the potential to, whereas I know I am absolutely safe with Lord Clitheroe."

"Have you ever wanted either of them to kiss you or hold you tighter during a waltz?" queried Kate. "Do you find either as attractive as they find you?"

"They are both good-looking men, are they not? But no, I have not wanted either of their kisses. I think perhaps that was left out of my makeup, Kate. I still have met no one who could convince me that my life would be better with him, than at home. And is there someone you wish to kiss?" she asked with a smile.

"No, not really." Kate wondered why a fleeting picture

of Lord Sidmouth bending down to touch his lips to hers
went through her mind at that moment. Probably because
they had been speaking of him and kisses in the same
breath. "But I do wish to be kissed. And loved. Do you not
feel envious when you see Arden and Gareth together?"

"I feel happy for them, and sometimes a little embarrassed when they touch in public. But not envious, no,"
replied Lynette.

"I feel sad for you, Lynnie. Here you are, the most beautiful woman in London this Season, and all you are looking
forward to is returning home to Yorkshire."

"There is nothing to feel sad about, Kate. If I wanted
something I couldn't have, that would be different. But
there is nothing that I want from a man. Perhaps one day
there will be, but not now."

Kate knew her sister was speaking the truth. And as
close as they were, here was this one part of Lynette that
she could not comprehend. It was not coldness, for Lynnie
was an affectionate sister and daughter. But desire seemed
to be missing from her makeup.

18

Although Lady Elizabeth and her husband were not as active as their daughters, they had been out often enough to enjoy their successes and to worry a little about the combined attentions of Lord Sidmouth and Lord Clitheroe.

One morning, when the younger members of the family had left for an early ride, Mr. Richmond and the dowager marchioness lingered at the breakfast table, discussing the girls' progress.

"Do you think either of them will receive an offer before the Season is over?" Mr. Richmond asked.

"The more pertinent question is whether either will accept one," the dowager replied.

Mr. Richmond raised his eyebrows. "Is Sidmouth serious then, do you think? He has been most persistent with Lynnette. And whom would you predict making an offer to Kate?"

"I think that both Sir Horace Granby and Mr. George Whitley are quite taken with Kate, Edward. By the end of the Season, one of them may very well come up to scratch."

"You are right. They have been hanging around. From all I know, either of them would be quite acceptable."

"Acceptable, yes—suitable for Kate is another question entirely."

"And Sidmouth?"

"Not at all suitable for Lynnette," replied the dowager. "And not likely to offer for her, I am afraid."

"What! With all the attention he has been paying her, he

damned well better not put her heart or her reputation in jeopardy!"

"Do you think her feelings are engaged then? I am not so sure, Edward."

"It is hard to tell with Lynette," he answered slowly. "She has been very friendly and receptive with Sidmouth."

"And with Clitheroe," the dowager pointed out. "And if either of the two would be likely to make an offer it would be Clitheroe."

"I must confess that I like him better and would think Lynette in very good hands."

The dowager smiled and nodded her agreement.

"I agree that Lord Clitheroe would be most appropriate for Lynette, and I have a great affection for him. But I must confess that I have a weakness for Lord Sidmouth," she said with a twinkle in her eye.

"I believe Elizabeth does too," said Edward.

"Ah yes, she knew his father who was as wild and charming a young man as his son. I remember the old marquess fondly myself."

"You don't sound very much like a Methodist to me, my dear Kate, confessing a weakness of a father-and-son pair of rogues," teased Mr. Richmond.

She laughed. "Do you know what amuses me most in this situation, Edward? The fact that if Clitheroe were to offer and Lynette to accept, the Otleys would be utterly overset by the family connection. His uncle is a bishop, you know, quite high up in the church hierarchy; a likely candidate for an archbishopric, as a matter-of-fact. And his mother! A rigid and controlling old trout. Can you imagine a family dinner with them? One polite inquiry about her scholarly interest and Lynette would scandalize the whole table."

"I never knew the Otleys that well. Are they really that bad?"

"I have always felt sorry for James. He is not really weak, but very imbued with loyalty to his family and their values. He inherited earlier than Sidmouth, and his mother managed to overdevelop his sense of what is due the title and family."

"Would he be the right sort of husband for Lynette then?"

"I think so, Edward. He is obviously not all Otley, or he would not have made such a good friend of Sidmouth. He would offset Lynette's tendency to escape into the world of scholarship, and his love for her might enable him to challenge the rigidity of his family."

"And what of Sidmouth? If he is not serious about Lynette, then what is he up to?"

"I do not think he is up to anything, Edward. His feverish pursuit of Lynette goes beyond wildness. The Harry Lifton who came home from the Peninsula is a different man than the one who left."

"Yet he seems to have recovered from his injuries, Kate," observed Mr. Richmond.

"I think his injuries went beyond the physical, Edward. And I also think," she continued in a lighter tone, "that he has chosen the wrong sister!" surprising both Mr. Richmond and herself by her spontaneous pronouncement.

But when she thought more about it later, the dowager decided that she was right. Whatever was driving the marquess, at heart she knew he was a good man, one who in a normal time, a time when young men were not exposed to the horrors of war, would never have put the heart of a young woman seriously at risk. If he were genuinely to fall in love with a woman, that woman's heart, she was sure, would be safe. And Kate had something to offer him: a down-to-earth quality that could balance his fey charm. It was a shame that neither of them seemed to see what was so obvious to her, now that she'd thought of it.

On the days that the dowager was about her work, she accepted no evening invitations. She merely sat back on those nights and enjoyed the sight of her sister-in-law and her nieces readying themselves for the current rout they were to attend.

This evening when Lynette came downstairs in her gown à la Grecque, the marchioness felt she was looking at her niece entirely differently, and a slight wave of anxiety went over her. Should they have been more concerned over the years about Lynette's retreat into scholarship? Was the young girl hidden away behind her startling beauty?

After her conversation with Edward, the marchioness was seized by a feeling of protectiveness, and had it not been so late, and she so tired, would have accompanied the family to their present engagement. She later wondered whether it would have made any difference at all in what occurred.

19

The evening started much as previous ones had. Young men rushed to fill Lynette's card, with Sidmouth and Clitheroe as always managing to be there for first choice. Kate's regular admirers and Lynette's overflow ensured her a successful evening also.

Lynette's first waltz was with Lord Clitheroe. By now he was very at ease with her. He was particularly pleased tonight, for he had managed to secure her company for supper also. They talked very little as they danced, but Lynette felt natural and relaxed in James's arms. He could still feel the reserve, but he had realized that it was more a part of her way of being than a particular reaction to him. And so he dared to hold her a little bit closer than was absolutely proper and to hold onto her hand just a little longer than necessary when the dance ended. Her smile and her "thank you" at the end were warm and genuine, and James walked away from her feeling more hopeful than he had in days. He didn't even feel his usual fit of annoyance as he watched Harry lead her out for the next country dance. A few more tunes, and he would have her company at supper.

It was a sultry evening for mid-April, and their dance had been quite lively. When Harry suggested that they seek a little more air than could be generated by a lady's fan, Lynette allowed him to lead her out onto one of the balconies.

She leaned over as though to drink in the air. "This is most refreshing, Lord Sidmouth. I am glad you suggested it. I fear I sometimes miss the climate of Yorkshire."

"Do the sights and sounds of London not compensate, Miss Richmond?" asked Harry, moving a bit closer.

"Oh, the city is certainly exciting, but after the novelty is gone, I find myself missing walks with Kate on the fell, and my work with my father."

"You have not spoken much about your work when I have been present, Miss Richmond."

Lynette smiled. "I have been warned, Lord Sidmouth. Not that I haven't been warned before, but this time I am determined to be on my best behavior so as not to ruin Kate's chances."

"And what about your own?"

"Oh, I am not looking for anything to develop out of this Season. I am happy to please my parents and sister, but I will be happy to be home again."

A few strands of hair had slipped out of Lynette's chignon, and Harry reached up and gently brushed them behind her ear. It was a quick, but intimate gesture, and he felt a slight shiver go through her. So she wasn't so indifferent after all, he thought.

"You are a very beautiful young woman, Miss Richmond, as I am sure you know. It would not be difficult for you to make a good match."

"I do not want to be married. And I especially do not want to be married merely for my beauty. It is an accident of birth, Lord Sidmouth." Lynette turned her face away and lifted it up to catch the breeze. In profile she was even more beautiful, and his eyes drank in the purity of line, in much the same way she drank in the cool air. Because hers was such an ethereal beauty, it was untouchable. And that was precisely why he wanted to touch her. He had waited long enough for his kiss, he decided, and moving behind her, he gently grasped her by the shoulder and turned her around toward him. Before she knew what was happening, he had trapped her chin with his hand and lightly kissed her on the mouth. Her eyes opened wide, and she tried to take a step back, but was stopped by the balcony railing. Harry smiled and traced her cheek with his finger and leaned down to kiss her again, this time longer and deeper. He wanted a response, he needed a response, and he lost himself in his own need. When she arched back, he took it as abandonment and opened her mouth with his tongue to make the kiss deeper. He was sure she wanted him. No woman he had ever kissed had resisted him. Underneath the angelic exterior was the responsiveness to his charm he had been counting on.

Lynette could feel the balcony pressing against her waist as she arched her back to get away from him. She was trapped. They were in the corner in the dark; there was no escape behind her and no one would come looking for her. Every cell in her body was screaming "Don't touch me, don't," but she seemed to have lost the power of speech. She finally summoned the strength and presence of mind to place her hands on Sidmouth's shoulders and push him away. She felt she was in a nightmare, the kind where you open your mouth and no screams come out, or you try to run and your feet won't move. Her arms felt like blancmange at first, but she was finally able to move him. Harry was ready to come up for air anyway, and he still was operating under the assumption that she wanted his kisses as much as he wanted hers. He knew, of course, that he would have to stop. He did not, after all, want to be caught in a compromising position and have to marry her.

When he finally realized she was intentionally holding him at arm's length, for the first time he really looked at her face. She was pale, not flushed with pleasure, and her eyes were wide with fear, not desire. She opened her mouth as though to speak or perhaps scream, but no sound came out. He pulled back at last and found himself stammering: "Miss Richmond, I . . ."

As soon as he let her go, Lynette slipped off the balcony. She immediately sought out her brother and his wife and hurried over to them, slipping her hand in Gareth's without even thinking. He looked down in surprise, for Lynette was not given to spontaneous gestures of affection, but he squeezed her hand and continued with conversation. She saw Sidmouth emerge from the balcony and start over to them, only to be waylaid by a friend who dragged him off in the other direction, to Lynette's great relief.

When Lord Clitheroe approached to lead her into supper, she smiled automatically and allowed him to take her arm and seat her and fill her plate. He chatted happily for a few minutes until he noticed that she was merely pushing her food around and hadn't tasted a bite.

"Are you feeling ill, Miss Richmond? You haven't even touched the lobster patties," he inquired solicitously.

Lynette lifted her eyes to his and nodded her head.

"You are ill! Here, let me take your plate and I'll get your sister."

Kate, who had been quietly chatting with Sir Horace came immediately. "Are you all right, Lynnie?"

Her sister just looked at her and shook her head and whispered "Home."

"You wish to go home? Of course." Kate turned to James. "Could you summon my brother and sister-in-law, Lord Clitheroe?"

"Certainly."

Kate clasped her sister's hands in hers. They were cold and damp. "Is it your stomach, Lynnie? You don't feel feverish."

"I don't know," replied her sister. "It is just a strange feeling that came over me all at once."

By the time they got her into the carriage, Lynette was shivering uncontrollably.

"Should we send for a doctor?" asked Gareth, as they helped her up the stairs and into the house.

Lynette shook her head and muttered through chattering teeth, "No, no doctor."

Kate sent one of the maids for a hot water bottle, which caused a flurry in the kitchen. On such a warm night, someone must be ill to need a hot water bottle.

But it was only that, two quilts, and her sister holding her in her arms that finally stopped Lynette's shaking.

"I am all right now," she whispered, and closing her eyes, she finally fell asleep. Kate stayed with her for a few minutes, but when it seemed clear that she really was sleeping at last, she tiptoed out of the room and quietly closed the door.

Her family was anxiously awaiting news downstairs. Lady Elizabeth was pacing in front of the fireplace, and when she heard Kate come in, she sat down at last and said, "What is it? A fever? Something she ate?"

"She did not seem unwell, Mother. At least, she had not been sick to her stomach. And she is not at all feverish. She just kept telling me that it was a feeling that she couldn't stop or really describe."

"Perhaps the excitement of the past few weeks has been too much for her," suggested Mr. Richmond. "We have all been going at a pace none of us is used to."

"I think that must be it," said Kate. "I can't think of anything else it might be. Unless she does develop a fever, I do not think we need to call a doctor."

"Well, I will make sure that she gets a few days of complete rest with no visitors and no obligations," declared Lady Elizabeth.

20

The next morning, when Lynette awoke, she felt as though she had been through a mangle. She closed her eyes and tried to remember the sequence of events from the evening before. Lord Sidmouth was kissing her, she was being bent back over a stone wall, and his hand was between her legs. . . . Her eyes flew open. Lord Sidmouth had kissed her, that was true enough. She had leaned back to get away from him. . . . She closed her eyes again and made herself remember. Her body felt the sensation of someone lifting her skirt, but the skirt was cotton, not silk. And then she heard Gabriel Crabtree's voice shouting, as though from a long distance, "Let her go, tha bastard, let t'lass go."

She opened her eyes again, and it was as though the ten-year-old Lynette were opening them. The strange feeling from the night before started to come back: where was she and how did she get here? She breathed deep into her stomach, and the feeling of panic began to recede. Something must have happened years ago, and Lord Sidmouth's advances had made her remember it. At the thought of Sidmouth, she shuddered. She could not imagine seeing him again. She had been right to be frightened of him. He had obviously had no sensitivity to her fear. Nay, he saw only what he wanted to see, based on his own responses. And his indifference to her feelings had brought her back to another time in her life when someone had used her, although she could not remember who.

Not only could she not imagine seeing Sidmouth again, she couldn't imagine continuing with the Season. The whole whirl of courting and being courted made her feel dizzy. She wanted to go home. She wanted to see Gabriel and find out from him whether she was crazy or remembering something that truly happened and he was somehow a part of it.

Having a purpose galvanized her, and she had just gotten out of bed when Kate opened her door slowly and peeked in.

"Lynnie! You get right back into bed."

Lynette smiled at her sister. "I feel much better, Kate, truly I do." But after pulling on her wrapper, she found herself wanting to sit down and sank into a chair.

Kate came over and held her hand against her sister's forehead. "You have no fever this morning either. That is a good sign. Perhaps Mother and Father are right, and it is just exhaustion from this mad pace we follow here in London."

"No, no, it isn't illness, Kate. It wasn't anything physical," Lynette started to say, and then color rushed to her cheeks.

"What is it, Lynnie? Whatever happened? The last time I saw you, you were dancing with Lord Sidmouth. The next thing I knew you had Gareth's hand and looked like a ghost. Wait a minute? Lord Sidmouth didn't frighten you in any way, did he?"

"We were out on the balcony to get some fresh air and he . . . kissed me," whispered Lynette.

"I will kill him for upsetting you so," said her sister.

"He only kissed me twice. I was trying to get away, but I couldn't. But now I am not sure it was really his fault, Kate." Lynette paused, not knowing how to explain, or even what there was to explain. Until she remembered fully, until she talked to Gabriel, how could she tell any of it. And even then, how could she speak of anything so shameful?

"Of course it was his fault. That rakeshame has been pursuing you since we arrived in London and is too sure of his own effect on women to even notice that you might not want his kisses. Wait until I see him. I will give him something to chew on, you can be sure."

Lynette protested weakly, feeling overwhelmed by all that had occurred. She didn't want to think about Sidmouth right now, she just wanted to go home. But she couldn't do that till she got a bit of strength back.

"I think I *will* spend the day in bed, Kate. But I am hungry."

"I'll have a light breakfast sent up to you, Lynnie. Now get back into bed."

After she settled her sister, Kate went downstairs, intent on ordering Lynette some food and then informing her parents what had happened. She was surprised to see the butler opening the door to an early caller and even more surprised to see it was Lord Clitheroe.

The butler was about to take his card and send him on his way when Kate stopped him. "No, Lester, I'll see Lord Clitheroe in the drawing room."

"Thank you, Miss Kate," said James. "I am sorry for calling so early, but I was so worried about your sister, that I came to inquire about her health. I hope it was nothing serious that sent her home early?"

"Sit down, Lord Clitheroe," said Kate, who remained standing. "I am very angry, my lord and I apologize ahead of time that I take it out on you. But your friend, Lord Sidmouth . . ."

"Yes?" James looked puzzled. What could Harry have to do with the situation?

"Lord Sidmouth took my sister out onto a balcony and quite overset her by mauling her against her will. I have had occasion myself to experience Lord Sidmouth's sudden violence, and I can quite understand Lynette's reaction."

"Harry attack an unwilling woman? That is very unlike him, Miss Kate."

"Lynette says he kissed her more than once and that she tried to get away but was trapped on the balcony."

The thought of Miss Richmond being so frightened by whatever Harry had done, frightened enough to become ill, enraged James. All the jealousy of the past weeks combined with his outrage that what he as a gentleman was bound to do was to convince his friend to offer for the woman he himself loved.

He stood up and, announcing that "He would be sure Lord Sidmouth would do the right thing," stalked out of the room without even a good-bye.

Kate looked blankly at the door closing behind him and wanted to run after him saying "No, it wasn't marriage she thought Lord Sidmouth needed to offer, but some sort of penance, like crawling up the fellside fifty times on his hands and knees."

"Gabriel should have left him to freeze to death," she muttered under her breath.

When James reached Harry's town house, the marquess was still asleep.

"No matter. I will wake him up," said James, pushing by the butler and taking the stairs two at a time. He threw Harry's door open and growled, "Get up, Harry, before I push you out of bed."

Lord Sidmouth, who had drunk more than usual in reaction to his belated realization that Lynette had not wanted his attentions, groaned at the noise. "James, whatever are you doing here at this ungodly hour?" he responded, pulling himself up on one elbow.

"I am here to get you dressed and over to the Richmonds', my lord, where you will make an offer for Miss Richmond within the hour."

"What!"

"You heard me. It is one thing to toy with a young lady's affection and then ignore her. It is quite another to assault an innocent."

"Assault! What in God's name are you talking about?"

"I am talking about whatever happened between you and Miss Richmond that made her feel ill enough to leave the ball early and has her confined to her bed at this moment."

A look of dismay and regret passed over Harry's face, and James was quick to notice it. He sank down into a chair, and said dully, "So you really did compromise her," all the anger and energy going out of him at once.

"James, I *did not* assault Miss Richmond. I took her out onto the balcony for a breath of air. I admit I kissed her once very gently, and then, when she did not make a protest, a little more passionately. But it was not more than I have done with other young ladies, I assure you, and no reason to call compromise. We were not out there so long as to be commented upon. And I thought she was enjoying my kisses until the last moment. I felt very bad about it. But when I heard she left early, I had no idea it had anything to do with me. I thought that she had truly been taken ill."

"Do you swear to that, Harry?"

"Should I have to, James?" his friend responded coldly.

"It is only that Miss Kate said that she too had experienced what she described as violence from you."

Harry was taken aback for a minute, and then replied in softer tones. "Miss Kate Richmond was indeed unfortunate enough to awaken me suddenly after that picnic we had on the fell. I responded as I would have to an enemy. I assure you, I do not bring that kind of violence into my dealings with women."

Harry looked pale under his tan, and his response was so serious that James believed him instantly.

"Thank God. I do not know what I am more relieved about—that you didn't hurt Miss Richmond or that you do not have to marry her."

Harry looked closely at his friend. "You really do love her then, James?"

James looked up at him bleakly. "Of course, you fool. What have you been thinking these past few weeks?"

"That you were only infatuated by her beauty, as I was. I judged you by my own lack of feeling, James. I am sorry."

"You should be. You put me through hell," responded James, with all the hostility he had been suppressing.

"Do you think your family will approve? The Richmonds are a bit odd, to say the least. What will your bishop uncle think about a connection with the Methodist Marchioness?"

"I have been a good and dutiful son all my life and done everything my mother wished of me. This time, I will do what I want. Except, of course, it won't matter, because

Miss Richmond has no more affection for me than she does for you."

"I am not sure Miss Richmond allows herself any great depth of feeling, James. That is what so fascinated me: the challenge of finally breaking through that remoteness. Well, I had better get dressed and go over there and make my apologies."

"Perhaps it would be better to wait until tomorrow, Harry. She was still confined to her bed today."

"All right. But join me for breakfast, James? I do not want you to leave with such bad feelings between us."

"I'll stay, Harry. I would like to clear the air."

21

K ate said nothing to her parents, for Lynette had sworn her to secrecy when she returned upstairs. Later in the morning, a small bouquet arrived, with a note attached, which Kate herself delivered to her sister.

"It is from Lord Sidmouth. I recognized his footman's livery," she said, holding the flowers out with a look of distaste on her face. "What a coward that he didn't come himself. I had thought Lord Clitheroe would persuade him."

"Lord Clitheroe? What does he know of this?" asked Lynette with a frown.

Kate looked a little shamefaced. "He called very early this morning, Lynnie, to see how you were. I am afraid I was so angry that I told him that Sidmouth had assaulted you."

"Kate, Lord Sidmouth did no more than kiss me. I told you that."

"But it must have been more, or you wouldn't have reacted that way."

A shadow passed over Lynette's face. She looked down at the note in her hand. "He has sent a sincere apology and has asked to call this afternoon to explain himself more fully. I can't see him, Kate. Not yet."

"Of course not. I will have Lester show him the door. Now get some sleep, Lynnie. You still look exhausted."

Lynette slept most of the morning and the early afternoon away. Kate satisfied the family by saying that her father was right: Lynette was just overcome by the frenetic activity of the last few weeks. And when Lord Sidmouth was announced, instead of having him sent away as she had originally planned, she told the butler to show the marquess into the drawing room.

After keeping him waiting a good fifteen minutes, she entered. Lord Sidmouth stood up and bowed, and then asked if it would be possible to have a few private words with her sister.

"I can assure you, my lord, that you have had more than enough time with my sister in private. She is sleeping at the moment, exhausted from her ordeal last night," replied Kate bitterly.

Harry had intended a sincere apology to Miss Richmond. He had never forced an unwilling woman and was ashamed of himself for frightening her and chagrined that he had misjudged her response. But he would hardly have called the kisses on the balcony an ordeal—especially for a scholar conversant with fertility symbols! Miss Kate Richmond made him lose all his good intentions, and he answered coldly, "Hardly an ordeal, Miss Kate. I was mistaken in my reading of your sister's response, nothing more."

"You forget, Lord Sidmouth, that I have experienced one of your assaults myself."

Harry flushed with anger and embarrassment. "Ah, yes, James told me you had flung that in his face. It is not at all comparable, and you know that. You had awakened a trained soldier out of a sound sleep. I am not violent with women, either in anger or love, I assure you," he said vehemently. "If Miss Richmond is asleep now, I will call tomorrow, for I would like the opportunity to personally explain to her my misreading of her response. Good day, Miss Kate." Harry got up, bowed, and left the room without a backward look, leaving Kate standing there with her mouth open.

When Lynette awoke later in the afternoon, she was surprised to find that she was ravenous. She decided that she would join the family for tea, and surprised all of them by appearing at the table.

"Lynette, my dear, I hope you are recovered," said her father.

Her mother immediately went over to her and felt her cheeks. "Cool as a cucumber," she announced with a smile. "Come, sit down, dear."

Lynette hated the fuss, but she had expected it, so she only smiled and explained that she did indeed seem to be recovering from her illness.

"Where are Gareth and Arden?" she asked after sitting down and being helped to a cup of tea. "And Aunt Kate?"

"Gareth and Arden are visiting friends, and Kate is out on her rounds this afternoon," replied her mother.

"Of course," Lynette murmured.

"Your mother and I have decided that you need a few days of complete rest. It is clear that this activity has been too much for you. May we send your regrets to your invitations?" asked Mr. Richmond.

"Why, yes, Father, perhaps that would be a good idea. I do not feel up to going out and about yet." Lynette was secretly relieved. She had spent some of her time in bed planning her way back to Yorkshire, and her only worry had been the embarrassment her family would suffer if she didn't appear at the various events they were invited to that week. This way, she wouldn't even be expected, and her absence would be explained away beforehand. "But you must not stay home for my sake yourselves. I hope you will go on with the week as planned."

"We will send regrets only for you, if you are sure, Lynette," said her mother. "I would not want to hold Kate back from the week's entertainments."

"Will you be riding with Gareth and Arden tomorrow, Kate?" her sister asked.

"Why, yes, Lynnie. I usually do on Wednesday morning."

Lynette was relieved. Her sister and brother would be gone, then, in the early morning. Her mother and father tended to sleep late. She had only one person to worry about, her aunt, whom she hoped would be tired enough from her work to sleep late also.

She went up early that evening and packed a few of her things in a small valise which she stuffed in the back of her closet. Luckily Gareth had been quite generous with pin money and she had more than enough to pay for the coach to York and a hired chaise from there to Hawes. She penned a short note, which she would leave propped up on her nightstand, explaining that she just couldn't face the rest of the Season and had returned home alone, so as not to ruin her family's enjoyment of it.

She had a few bad moments as she slipped into bed, wondering whether this was the right thing to do. What would she say to Gabriel, after all, to get him talking? And was there anything to talk about? Maybe she had just had a nightmare once upon a time and Lord Sidmouth's kisses brought it back? At the thought of Lord Sidmouth and his pending visit, she shivered. No, one good reason for leaving was that she couldn't face seeing him again. She was embarrassed, ashamed, and afraid, all three at once, and right now, he was the cause of all those feelings. No, she would slip out tomorrow morning and be on her way home before anyone even missed her.

Aunt Kate did sleep late the next morning, as did her parents, so as soon as she heard Kate and the others leave, she dressed quickly, checked to make sure her note would be seen, and slipped out the French doors leading to the garden. It was only a short walk from the back entrance to a hackney stand, and she easily made the coach to York. She was on the road for a good two hours before anyone did miss her.

Her maid had entered quietly, intending to ask if she wanted her chocolate in bed and was surprised to see the bed made and Lynette not sitting in the chair by the window, reading, as she was wont to do in the morning. Martha would not have been overly concerned had she not spied the cream-colored square resting on the nightstand. She slipped out and went to knock gently on the dowager marchioness's door.

"Yes, who is it?"

" 'Tis Martha, my lady. There is something I think you should know."

The dowager came to the door, her gray hair in its overnight braid, pulling her wrapper closed. Martha had been with her for years, and she knew that "something" must be serious for her maid to disturb her like this.

"What is it, Martha?"

"'Tis the young lady, mum. Miss Richmond. She is not in her room."

"Surely she is just down to breakfast early then?"

"No, my lady. And there looks to be a note, or else I wouldn't have disturbed you."

The dowager finished tying her wrapper and led the way down the hall. She sat on Lynette's bed and fingered the folded paper for a moment, looking around at the state of the room. It showed no sign of upset, but that worried her even more. If Lynette had gone off somewhere, then she had been thinking about it beforehand. The note, when she finally opened it, confirmed her suspicions.

"Oh, dear," she sighed.

"I hope the young lady is all right. Not kidnapped or anything?"

"No, Martha, this is not a ransom demand," said the dowager with a smile, "though I know that would make more exciting gossip belowstairs."

"I would never, my lady!"

"I know, Martha, I was only teasing you. Although I do need you to make a few inquiries amongst the other servants. Perhaps someone saw her leave and could tell us when."

Martha curtsied and hurried off to the kitchen. Things were usually very calm in the Thorne household, and it was nice to have a little excitement, although she certainly would not wish any harm to that sweet Miss Richmond.

22

The dowager looked at the note in her hand again. All Lynette said was that she was tired from the strain of the Season, and not wishing to spoil anyone else's plans had decided to slip off by herself and return home. But why wouldn't she have just told her parents or Gareth? Was it only fatigue or was it something else?

She heard laughing and chattering as Gareth and the others returned from their ride. Kate's room was next to her sister's, so the dowager waited until she had entered, and then knocked on the door and opened it without waiting for an invitation to come in.

"Aunt Kate! Good morning. I am just changing for breakfast," said her niece.

"Kate, Lynette is gone."

"Gone? What do you mean? Gone where?"

"According to this note," said the dowager, handing it over to her niece, "she has gone home to Yorkshire."

"Damn Sidmouth!" said Kate, without thinking.

"Sidmouth? What has he got to do with this?"

"I promised I wouldn't tell, but I suppose this changes things," said Kate. "Lord Sidmouth attacked Lynette the other night at the ball."

"Harry Lifton? I would not have believed it of him."

"Well, to do him justice, both he and Lynnie denied it was an assault, exactly. But why else would she have fled back home?"

"Tell me exactly what you know, Kate."

"Well, Lynnie told me that Lord Sidmouth took her out

on the balcony, supposedly for a breath of air, and then
kissed her against her will. More than once."

"A kiss or two is hardly an attack, my dear."

"She was unwilling, and he ignored that. He says he
thought she wanted him to. At any rate, whatever happened, it upset her so much that she was ill for a day and
now has run off to escape him."

"There must be something else to this that we don't
know, Kate. Do your parents know about Sidmouth?"

"No, Lynnie didn't want anyone else to know, for she
was too upset and embarrassed. The only other person who
knows is Lord Clitheroe."

"Well, we must talk to Edward and Elizabeth and then
decide what to do."

"Why, go after her, of course."

"I don't know if that is the best thing to do. She did have
enough money?"

"I am sure she did. Gareth has been very generous, Aunt
Kate."

"Lynette has done enough traveling with your father that
she can take care of herself. I admit, I don't like the idea of
a young woman traveling alone, but I doubt she is in any
real danger."

"But we can't just let her run off like that," protested
Kate.

"It is not a question of 'let,' my dear. She is already on
her way. Come, let us wake your parents, and decide as a
family what is best to be done."

The Richmonds had only begun their conversation when
Lord Clitheroe was announced.

"Tell him Lynette is still not well and send him away,
Lester," said Lady Elizabeth, before the butler could finish
his sentence.

"Lord Clitheroe did not ask for Miss Richmond, my
lady. He is desirous of speaking with Mr. Richmond."

Lady Elizabeth raised her eyebrows at this and looked
over at her husband inquiringly. "Edward?"

"I think I will see him, my dear. Show him into the library, Lester. I will be with him in a moment."

"I think we can all guess what Lord Clitheroe has to say, Papa," said Kate. "But what an awkward time for him to come courting. Whatever will you tell him?"

"The truth, Kate. He deserves that if he indeed is here to ask for Lynette's hand. Whether he wants to pursue his suit further is up to him, once he discovers that she has gone home. My opinion, by the way, is for us to leave her alone," concluded Mr. Richmond, as he walked out the door.

"Good morning, Lord Clitheroe."

James, who had been aimlessly browsing through the books on the table in front of him, jumped up to greet Mr. Richmond.

"Please sit down, my lord. You wished to speak with me?"

"You may have guessed why, sir. You cannot be ignorant of my interest in your daughter. I would like your permission to court her."

Mr. Richmond smiled. "I could hardly miss your interest in Lynette, and am pleased by it. Tell me, Lord Clitheroe, do you have any reason to believe that my daughter would welcome your suit?"

James blushed. "No, not any real reason, Mr. Richmond. I can say only that she seems to enjoy my company."

"More than any other of her admirers?"

"I really couldn't say. But I can tell you that I have not clearly presented myself as a suitor before now. That is, I have sought Miss Richmond out, and she is surely aware that I am interested in her. But I have held myself back from any open courting."

"Like kisses on the balcony?"

"You know about Sidmouth then?" asked James quietly. "He would be here instead of me, had I thought he had compromised her. In fact, I visited him yesterday to inform him that he would propose marriage or meet me at dawn."

"Even though you wish to marry her?"

"I wrongly assumed that Harry must have gone further than a kiss or two, when I heard Miss Richmond had left early. When I confronted him, however, he assured me that he had misread her reaction."

"Are you also here to apologize for your friend, Lord Clitheroe?" asked Mr. Richmond with a touch of irony.

"Not at all. Harry can apologize for himself. No, it was just that it was the visit to Harry that clarified my feelings. He does not love your daughter, Mr. Richmond. I do. And I feel ready to communicate that to her."

"Unfortunately, Lynette is on her way home to Yorkshire."

"What? If Sidmouth lied to me, I'll kill him," said James.

"There is no reason to believe your friend a liar. Lynette's account of the incident to her sister matches Lord Sidmouth's exactly."

James let out a sigh of relief. "But why then has she left London?"

"We really don't know, Lord Clitheroe. We lead a very quiet life in Yorkshire, and Lynette and I are rather reclusive. It may be that the strain of all this socializing has been building, and Sidmouth's behavior was just enough to push her over the edge." Mr. Richmond hesitated a moment before going on. "Tell me, Lord Clitheroe, have you even attempted a kiss?"

James looked down at his boots as thought he were hoping he could see himself in their high shine and find out what kind of fellow this was who let all opportunities to woo his lady pass him by. "Well, no. Not really. I have held Miss Richmond a little closer than one should during the waltz and squeezed her hand. But I have always felt some wall there, and I never wanted to take the besieger's route. I suppose I was hoping that persistence and patience would eventually cause Miss Richmond to let the wall down herself."

Mr. Richmond smiled. "Lynette can seem like the maiden in the tower, can't she? Hers is not so much a sensuous beauty as an otherworldly one."

James blushed. "I think Harry found her remoteness tantalizing."

"And you, Lord Clitheroe?"

"I wish to know Miss Richmond herself. I must admit that her beauty amazed me the first time I saw her. But what I find irresistible is the sense of the real woman hidden behind that face."

"Yes, Lynette has always felt to me like a 'sleeping beauty,' Lord Clitheroe. Some part of her is unawakened. Or has been until now."

"I had wanted it to be *my* kiss," said James, with quiet anger. "And it is too late now."

"Oh, I wouldn't say that, James. I may call you James? After all, we hope to be related," added Mr. Richmond with a smile.

"Then you do approve of my suit?"

"I think you are just what Lynette needs. You are steady and honorable, and very down-to-earth. She will drive you to distraction at times, you know, with her absentmindedness and total absorption in her studies. I know I do the same to Lady Elizabeth."

"Oh, no, never," protested James. "I admire her intellect."

Mr. Richmond grinned. "Believe me, James, she will. But if you love each other, that won't matter."

"But she doesn't love me," James protested.

"Not yet. But then, up until now, she wouldn't have been likely to love anyone. But something has happened because of Sidmouth, I am sure, although I have no idea what it could be to send her back to Yorkshire without speaking to us."

"Will you all return home now?"

"Oh, no, not at all. In fact," declared Mr. Richmond, "I am going to send you after her. Oh, not right away. We need to give her a day or two at home. But I think you need to make your interest as clear to Lynette as you have to me."

"You mean propose to her?"

"Perhaps not that immediately. But tell her you have my

permission to court her. And ask hers. And get her back down to London, James," he added with a rueful laugh. "For we have only a short time before May Eve, and I want her with me in Padstow!"

23

Lynette arrived home in Sedbusk just after dark. She gave the hired driver his pay and directed him back to the inn at Hawes. Picking up her bag, she looked around her, drinking in the fresh smell of grass. It was good to be home again, away from the smoke and fog of London and the mad whirl of the last few weeks. She would have to face what had brought her home, but not until morning, she decided, and knocked on the front door, hoping that Janie was still there.

It took a minute or so for Janie to answer, and when she did, she peeked out and asked sharply who was there.

"It is me, Janie. Lynette."

"Miss Lynnie! Whatever art tha doing here, lass? Tha's supposed to be in London."

At the sound of Janie's soft Yorkshire voice, Lynette felt tears come to her eyes.

"It was all too much for me, Janie. Are you going to invite me in?"

Janie pulled her into her arms and gave her a big hug. "Tha'rt lucky tha caught me here. I had just fed t'cat and t'stable lad and was on my way home to my own dinner. Coom into the parlor and I'll light t' fire."

The journey from London had been tedious and tiring and it was very good to be taken care of after two days of strange inns.

"There is only eggs and bacon, lass, and soom day-old bread."

"That sounds wonderful, Janie."

Lynette surprised herself by eating ravenously. She

hadn't wanted food since the evening Lord Sidmouth had kissed her. But the warmth and safety of home relaxed her and she more than did justice to Janie's supper.

"Did tha coom alone?"

"Yes. I was finding it all a bit overwhelming, but I didn't want to spoil anything for Kate."

"And do tha parents know tha'rt here, lass?" asked Janie.

"Yes, Janie," Lynette said, smiling at the woman's stern tone.

"And they let tha travel alone?"

"I left them a note," Lynette confessed. "I just needed to come home."

"Now, now, tha is here and safe. But that must send them a letter, telling them tha arrived."

"I'll do that tomorrow."

"I have to leave, lass, and go home and cook supper for my George. But I do not like leaving tha alone."

"I won't be alone, Janie. I'll have Mott, and Jake is right over the stable. I will be fine, truly."

"If tha is sure, I will go now and be back early in t'morning."

"Thank you, Janie."

"Good night, lass, and welcome home."

Lynette stayed by the fire for a while, watching the flames die down. Mott had jumped into her lap as soon as she finished eating and was purring loudly, happy to have a member of the family home. "Coom on, tha great beast," she crooned, as she draped him over her shoulder, and picking up a lamp, climbed the stairs to her own room. She deposited him at the foot of the bed, knowing that by morning he would be curled up next to her, and slipping out of her dress and into a nightrail, crawled under the covers and was asleep in minutes.

The next morning she was awakened by Mott, who had jumped onto her chest and was peering into her face.

"Tha's a great pain in the arse, tha mangy cat," muttered Lynette. "Aye, and tha only understands broad Yorkshire, eh? Oh Mott, it is good to have your company, even though you are exactly what I called you!"

But Mott had done his job, which was to wake her up. He was not in the mood for cuddling, and so he jumped off the bed and stalked to the door, giving her one look over his shoulder before he went out.

Lynette pulled on her wrapper and stood by the window, looking out over the pastures and up toward the scree. It was a sunny morning and looked to remain so. It was therefore a good day to seek out Gabriel, and as she remembered why she came, she gave an involuntary shiver. She had managed to put it out of her mind as soon as she boarded the coach, but now she had to think about it. Something more than Sidmouth's kisses had brought on that awful, nameless feeling, and Gabriel most probably held the key. She pulled on her most comfortable walking dress and went down to breakfast.

Janie was there, eager to hear all about the great ladies and gentlemen she had met, and so Lynette described an evening out in London, from the crush of carriages at the door of a great house to the blazing ballrooms and lavish suppers.

"And tha waltzed, lass?"

"Yes, Janie, many times."

"Has tha waltzed with that nice Lord Clitheroe?"

"Yes, Janie," Lynette answered with a faint blush.

"Good. He would make a fine husband for tha, Miss Lynnie."

"Janie! I am not looking for a husband. And I have no idea whether Lord Clitheroe is looking for a wife."

"Tha might not be looking, lass. But tha needs one. And I saw the way he looked at tha."

"I do not want to sound conceited, Janie, but you know I am often admired for my looks. That does not mean a declaration of marriage is soon to follow."

"I know tha face draws them like moths to a flame, lass. But Lord Clitheroe is different, I'd be willing to wager."

"Lord Clitheroe was attentive, but no more so than others."

"Oh, aye, I bet t'other one was. Now he would *not* make tha a good husband."

"Lord Sidmouth! Hardly."

"But he might make Miss Kate one," added Janie thoughtfully.

"Lord Sidmouth and Kate? Why they almost seem to dislike each other!"

"Aye, lass. Well, that is the way it often begins. My George and I could barely stand the sight of each other at first."

"Janie, I didn't know you have taken up matchmaking in your old age," teased Lynette.

"I know tha and tha sister as well as anyone, my lass, and I have a good idea of what sort of man would suit tha. And it was no accident that those two arrived here. It was meant, mark my words."

"And now you sound like a fortune-teller!"

"Tha just wait and see, lass."

Lynette found herself smiling over Janie's predictions as she walked up the path toward Gabriel's hut. Lord Sidmouth and Kate, indeed. And then the thought of Sidmouth wiped the smile off her face. The path she took was next to one of the low stone walls that marked one pasture from another. She ran her hand over the top as she walked and wondered about her memory, if that's what it was, of being pushed back against a wall just like it.

When she got to the hut, the old shepherd was already gone, which meant she had to climb farther. She hoped that he had not ranged too far today, for she had no energy to wander from pasture to pasture.

She was almost halfway up to the scree when she heard a dog barking. Hoping it was Benjamin, she headed in the direction of the sound and was relieved to see Gabriel leaning on his staff and watching the dog drive two sheep down from the top.

"Gabriel," she called.

He turned, completely surprised by her call.

Lynette waved and climbed quickly, so that she was beside him almost before he recognized her.

"Miss Lynnie! Whatever art tha doing here? Tha is in London."

"Now, how could I be here and in London at the same time," she teased.

"Hast t'family coom back?"

"No, Gabriel. The rest of them are still in the city."

"Is soomthing wrong, lass, that tha left? Were tha not asked to waltz enough waltzes," said Gabriel, laughing his raspy laugh. "Or did tha scandalize soomone with tha heathen studies?"

"Gabriel!"

"Aye, well, I may not be at t'assemblies, lass, but I hear t'gossip. Tha'rt a rare one for drawing them in and then shocking them off."

"I was very well behaved in London," replied Lynette. "I never even uttered the word 'fertility,' I'll have you know."

"Then why hast tha coom back?"

"To see you, Gabriel," Lynette answered in a very different tone.

"To see this dirty old shepherd, when tha has all the dooks in London after tha?"

"Gabriel, something happened when I was in London. I was . . . I am not sure how to explain this. Is there some place we can sit down?"

"Coom over to t'rocks, lass. I'll spread my coat out to keep tha clean."

Lynette smiled to herself at that. The rocks were likely to be cleaner than Gabriel's old coat. But she thanked him and sank down gratefully on one of the boulders that studded the scree. Gabriel perched next to her and peered down.

"Na then, lass, what happened to tha?"

"Do you remember Lord Sidmouth?"

Gabriel looked blank.

"Harry Lifton. The man you and Benjamin rescued."

"Oh, aye, t' young soldier. I forgot he were a lord."

"A marquess. He was very attentive to me in London."

"Aye, and not t'only one, I wager."

"But the most persistent. He took me out on a balcony a few nights ago. We had been dancing, and it was quite warm and we wanted some fresh air. And he kissed me," she added, with her eyes lowered in embarrassment.

"Did tha not want him to, lass?"

"No."

"And did he stop?"

"No."

Gabriel struck the ground with his staff. "Mayhap Benjamin and I should not have rescued him after all. I would not have thought him to be that sort."

"To be honest, Gabriel, I don't think he is. He thought I was enjoying it."

"And tha wasn't at all?"

"Something happened, Gabriel. I was bending back over the railing to get away, and he was leaning over me and kissing me harder and all of a sudden ... a horrible feeling came over me. And when I tried to figure it out later at home, I remembered. It was as though I was here, and you were here, too. You were shouting to someone to let me go." Lynette's voice was shaking, and it took all her courage to look up at Gabriel. "Was I only remembering a nightmare, do you think? Or did something happen?"

Gabriel placed his hand on top of hers and looked down at the ground in front of him. His face, which was reddened from all the years spent outdoors, was even redder from the embarrassment of having Miss Lynnie talking to him about things he shouldn't be hearing.

" 'Twas no nightmare, lass," he finally got out.

"Then someone did do something to me? Was it when I was about nine or ten, Gabriel?"

Gabriel's hand clenched over hers, and she winced with the pain.

"I am sorry, lass," he said when he realized what he had done. "I am not sure I can tell tha."

"I must know, Gabriel. Please don't be embarrassed for me."

" 'Twere Thomas Halloch."

As soon as he said the name Lynette shuddered, and she

immediately saw the flushed face, smelt the bad breath of Thomas Halloch, a shepherd who had worked for them for a short time. It came back in that instant, as though his name were the key to it all. His name and Gabriel's voice.

24

She had been almost ten that summer. She'd been a great reader, even then, and as different from Kate as she was now. Kate, when she played, was likely to play in the barn with the new kittens or ride the fat old pony their father had bought them, or tag along with Gareth. Lynnie joined her sometimes, but what Lynnie most liked to do was pretend. Sometimes she would have Kate act out a scene with her from the Robin Hood ballads. In fact, one time they were sent to their rooms supperless when they came home dripping wet after acting out Robin and Little John's fight on the log bridge. Lynnie, being the taller one, was Little John.

On that particular morning, however, Lynnie had been Gareth, setting out to rescue Lynette, their father having passed on his love for the Arthurian cycle to her. She was never a lady when she pretended, not even when the lady in the story bore her name. No, she wanted adventure. She had gotten up at dawn, thrown an old cloak over her, grabbed bread and cheese from the kitchen, and was out before the sun began to burn off the early morning mist.

Everything was dripping with moisture. It was wonderful to be out on such a fog-enshrouded morning, before anyone else was stirring, and she was so caught up in being Gareth that the shape that came out of the mist seemed to be only a creature of her imagination. Until he stopped her by grabbing her arm.

He said nothing, and perhaps that was the worst of all. She was walking along, completely absorbed in her "rescue," and then, suddenly, rough hands were pushing her back against the stone wall. Someone's mouth was over hers, pushing her lips open.

They were well out of sight of the house, and with his mouth covering hers, she couldn't make a sound. To her horror, his hand went between her legs, as though drawn there by a magnet. She wondered what she could have done, that he would touch her there. She almost fainted with relief when he moved it away, only to realize that he was fumbling with her dress, pushing it over her hips so that he could reach under it. His fingers found her most private part, and as he tried to push them into her, she gasped with the pain.

It was then that she screamed, and through the fog saw another shape approaching. At first she thought it was the man's companion, but when she heard him shout, she realized it was Gabriel.

"Let her go, tha bastard, let t'lass go."

Halloch pulled back from her, as surprised as she was at the apparition, for so Gabriel seemed, emerging from the mist.

He was on her attacker in a moment, pulling him off Lynette, and leveling him with one blow to the chin. Lynette looked down, as though from a great distance at the man writhing at her feet. Gabriel was beating him about the shoulders with his staff, using words that Lynette had never heard before. Just as Gabriel lifted his staff and looked ready to drive it down the man's throat, Lynette reached out.

"No, Gabriel, no. You'll kill him."

A great shudder went through the old shepherd, and he lifted the staff slowly. Halloch rolled out from under the poised weapon and half crawled, half ran down the fellside. Gabriel turned to her and she almost fell against him.

"Art tha all reet, lass? He didn't harm tha, did he?"

"No, he only kissed me," said Lynette, when she could speak.

"Art sure?"

Lynette could not, would not tell of that hand seeking out her private self. She could not tell Gabriel, and she could not ever imagine telling her parents, ever in her life. For if she told them, they would look at her and know that it was something in herself, in Lynnie, that had drawn his hand *there*.

"Let me get tha home and we will tell tha parents. They'll have the sheriff on him for sure."

"No, Gabriel, please don't."

"What does tha mean, lass. Of course I have to tell tha father."

"No, Gabriel, please," she begged. "I am sure Halloch will never show his face around here again. I cannot tell anyone. It is too shameful."

Gabriel protested, but Lynette became half-hysterical, and so he gave in. She had gone through enough, and he was afraid to put her through any more. And likely in a few days when she had gotten over it, she would tell her parents herself.

"I will bring tha down to t'house, lass. And tha must promise never to coom out alone like this again."

Lynette nodded her agreement, and Gabriel led her to the back door.

"Art sure tha'rt all reet now?"

"Yes, Gabriel. And thank you." Lynette gave the old shepherd such a look of gratitude, that he thought his heart would crack within him when she turned and squaring her small shoulders, walked into the house alone.

"I was never sure I did reet, lass, not telling tha father."

"It was the right thing to do, Gabriel. Truly, I could not have borne their questions."

"And did tha not remember from then to now, lass?" he asked wonderingly.

"I must have pushed it out of my mind almost immediately, Gabriel. And it was only Lord Sidmouth's behavior and the feeling of the balcony railing against my back that reawakened the memory."

"I'd like to get my hands on that young man then."

"No, he really did do no more than kiss me, you know.

Perhaps, in some strange way, he did me a favor, for he woke up a part of me that has been asleep for many years."

Gabriel looked over and saw the tears streaming down Lynette's face. He put his arm around her and drew her close. "Ah, lass, do not grieve thaself over this. It all happened so long ago."

"But I still feel that it was somehow my fault, Gabriel. I should not have gone out so early. I must have done something, at some time, to give him the idea that I would welcome such behavior . . . "

"Nay, lass," said Gabriel sternly, grasping her shoulders and looking into her eyes. "Tha was on tha father's farm. Why should tha not be able to walk it safely. Halloch was a . . . Well, I cannot say it in front of tha."

"But you did then," said Lynette, smiling at last. "You called him all sorts of terrible names, Gabriel," she said with a teary laugh. "And you nearly killed him. I can see you, standing over him with your staff, ready to crush his throat."

"I wish I had, lass. I would have, too, had I known he would cause tha this pain."

"Part of me wishes you had, too," she said fiercely. "But you looked like St. George killing the dragon. You came to my rescue, just like a knight of old."

"Soom knight, Miss Lynnie!" replied Gabriel with a snort. "But Halloch was indeed a lowly worm, that is t'truth."

"Gabriel, I feel so different," said Lynette, so softly he almost didn't catch her words.

"How is that, Miss Lynnie?"

"I don't know. More . . . real. Or perhaps it is that everything around me is more real."

And it was true. The rock was solid beneath her bottom, and she could feel the sharp edge of it cutting into her thigh. She was breathing in fresh air and Gabriel's pungent smell, all at once. She gently pulled herself away and looked over at her "knight." He sat there, a grizzled old Yorkshireman with huge hands that could have crushed the life out of Thomas Halloch, but which also could soothe a frightened lamb. He smelled a unique Gabriel-smell, composed of sheep, dog, sweat, and smoke. And he had tufts of gray hair growing out of his ears. She had never noticed that before.

He patted her shoulder awkwardly. "Tha should not pull away from young men just because of what happened, tha knows. Tha'rt young and beautiful, Miss Lynnie. And loving."

"Am I, Gabriel? Oh, I know I am beautiful. But am I a loving person?" she asked with a catch in her throat.

"Oh, I remember tha with t'lambs. And with tha sister, Kate, when tha were both small. Tha wa always watching over her."

Lynette felt something loosen inside her. Gabriel had given her back something she had lost years ago. It was that young girl, Lynnie. She *had* been a loving child. She had opened her arms wide to her sister, her brother, her family. And she had lost that little girl because she had been terrified. Terrified that that man knew something about her. Knew that she was loving. Knew that she was passionate about the world around her. Knew that she was vulnerable. He had wanted that little girl, for what she wasn't sure. But he had wanted her, and Lynette, terrified, had hidden her away so no one could want her for those reasons again.

25

Lynette stayed while Gabriel brought the ewes down to the lower pasture. Benjamin came over to them after his work was done, tail wagging and mouth open in a grin of delight.

"T'old dog is happy to see thee, lass."

Lynette sank to her knees and hugged the dog to her, laughing as he licked her face.

"Wilt coom back down for a cup of tea, lass?"

"Some other time, Gabriel. I had best get back to the house in time for dinner, or Janie will be worried. Thank you again, my good friend."

Gabriel patted her shoulders clumsily, embarrassed by the reminder. He watched her make her way down the path and said to Benjamin, "I wonder if it were a good or a bad thing, lad, that we rescued those two? Only time will tell, eh?"

After dinner Lynette went into the library, thinking that she might do a bit of work on her father's book. As she paged through his manuscript and looked at the prints and drawings he had included, for the first time she was able to see them from an outsider's point of view, and realized how she had been hiding behind her scholarship. And how ironic that she, who was so clearly afraid of a man's touch, should be quite comfortable researching fertility rites! It was as though by using her mind to investigate one aspect of the sensual life, she could avoid all real experience. Now, for the first time in her life, she found herself blushing at the *sheela-na-gigs*, the female exhibitionists. Yet, at the same time, looking at them helped her, for while they were shocking they also were strong. And she needed to believe that allowing herself to be a passionate woman was not dangerous.

She spent only a short time with the manuscript before she was overcome by an overwhelming wave of fatigue, and she stumbled up to bed and fell asleep immediately.

She slept for more than two hours and realized it was getting close to teatime when she awoke. She was lying there, listening to Janie bustling away in the kitchen when she was startled by the sound of a horse coming up the drive. The neighbors think we are all in London, so who would be visiting at this time of day, she wondered.

She heard the knocker and Janie's greeting, and a deeper voice answering. She got up and splashed water on her face and, brushing the tangles out of her hair, tied it quickly back in a knot. Perhaps her family had sent someone after her, she thought as she walked downstairs. Janie was back in the kitchen, so Lynette peered into the parlor and almost ran back upstairs when she saw Lord Clitheroe seated by the fire, watching Mott, who was stalking round and round his chair, giving him threatening looks from his huge orange eyes.

Lynette smiled. Lord Clitheroe had sat himself down in Mott's chair and was going to regret it when he got up and found his trousers covered with cat hairs. But her amusement was only momentary, for Clitheroe must have heard her come in. He turned and stood up immediately, giving Mott the opportunity he'd been waiting for. In one second the cat was curled up on the warm cushion.

"Miss Richmond."

"Lord Clitheroe. Are you visiting the neighborhood?" Lynette felt silly asking him that, but why else was he here? "Please sit down. Oh, not there," she warned, as Clitheroe was about to sit on Mott. "I am afraid you will have to yield that chair to the cat."

James looked down and barely saved himself. He moved to the sofa, and as Lynette sat opposite him, sank down.

"To answer your question, Miss Richmond, I have come to see you."

"Me?" Lynette was afraid to hear why. Lord Sidmouth and Lord Clitheroe were such good friends. Could Sidmouth have sent him with some sort of message?

"Yes, for several reasons. First, I am here to apologize for Lord Sidmouth's behavior."

"Shouldn't Lord Sidmouth be doing that himself?" she asked, with an edge to her voice.

"Under different circumstances, he would have."

"To be quite fair to Lord Sidmouth," added Lynette in a low voice, "his offense was only misreading my response."

"I am glad to hear that," replied James, who although he felt quite guilty about his lack of trust in Harry, had had a lingering doubt about his friend's account.

"But how did you know how to find me?"

"Your family told me when I called that you had come home," James informed her.

"Does all London know?" asked Lynette with a painful smile.

"As a matter of fact for this week they have put the word out that you were exhausted and that the doctor ordered complete rest. For now, as far as the *ton* knows, you are still in London."

"I see. And next week? When I don't return?"

"I was hoping . . . that is, your father and mother were hoping that you would return. And I was to give you a special reminder from your father that May Day is only a little more than two weeks away. Although, I confess, I don't know what bearing that has on anything." James grinned. "He mentioned something about a hobby horse and Padstow?"

Lynette's face lit up with one of the few genuine smiles James had ever seen from her. "Only my father would know what might draw me back!"

James cleared his throat nervously. "Now that I have delivered those messages, I have my own reason for being here."

Lynette looked at him inquiringly.

"I have asked your father for his permission to pay my

addresses to you, and he has granted it. That is, of course, the only reason they let me come after you."

Lynette said nothing, and James rushed nervously to fill in the silence. "I am not actually proposing marriage yet, Miss Richmond."

"I am glad, for I would hate to refuse you," she answered softly.

"I wanted you to know, however, that I want to get to know you better and have you come to know me . . . so that, if I did propose, there might be a chance in the future you would say yes. I wanted it to be clear that I have, as you might say, 'come a-courting,' " James finished on a humorous note.

"I have truly never thought of marrying, Lord Clitheroe."

"I have heard you say that before. But perhaps you might begin to think of it as a possibility?"

"Lord Clitheroe, I am going to say something that will sound immodest, nay, egotistical, but I must say it. I am a beautiful woman, and that beauty draws men to me. Lord Sidmouth was one of them. But that beauty has nothing to do with the real me. Perhaps you have fallen in love only with my face. Perhaps you wish to have a beautiful wife? You do not really know Lynette Richmond, so how could you want to marry her?"

"No, I do not. And that is why I have not asked you to marry me. For now, I wish to come to know the real you. And to have you get to know me. I am plain-spoken, Miss Richmond, not charming, like Harry."

"That is a point in your favor, Lord Clitheroe," said Lynette with a smile.

"I have never felt that you disliked me or found my attentions distasteful."

"Of course not. I do like you. I just have not thought of you romantically. But then," continued Lynette, as though she were speaking to herself, "I have never let myself consider any man that way."

"Can I convince you to at least begin to think of me in that light?"

"I cannot promise you anything, Lord Clitheroe. I do not want to hurt you . . . "

"You need promise nothing more than that you will take me seriously as a friend and possible suitor."

Lynette looked at James's face. It was absolutely open and vulnerable. His eyes did not burn with desire, as Sidmouth's had. Sidmouth's desire had blinded him to her own lack of it. James's eyes were clear and looking straight at her, wanting to know what *she* felt, what *she* wanted. She did not feel backed against a wall by the force of another's need. She felt afraid, it was true, but a different kind of fear. James (for that was how she was beginning to think of him), was inviting her into his feelings, inviting her to lower the barrier she had raised years ago, inviting her out into the real world, where joy was as much a possibility as pain and disappointment.

She could say no, of course. But she found she didn't want to. She wanted to know James better. And she wanted him to get to know her better. And, she suspected, if both those things happened, she would get to know herself.

She lowered her eyes. "I would like to have you as a friend, my lord."

"And perhaps later as a suitor?" James held his breath.

"Perhaps."

Thank God Janie appeared with a tea tray at that moment, for James was speechless. He had not really expected to be successful. He was, aside from his wealth and title, nothing very special. And yet Miss Richmond was going to give him a chance.

From the charged silence, Janie knew that something was in the air, and she chatted away to ease the tension. Finally Lynette and James were able to offer commonplaces to each other, and Janie could get back to the kitchen without worrying that they would sit there in dead silence.

"I will be staying at the inn tonight," said James as he slathered jam on one of Janie's hot scones. "But I will be available to escort you back to London whenever you wish."

"I had better return right away," Lynette replied. "One

week of exhaustion is believable, but if I stay away longer they'll have to come up with another explanation."

"Your father sent some money along in case you needed it. I imagine we could hire a chaise in Hawes?"

"Yes."

"But you will need an abigail, of course. I will ride outside, but we don't want any gossip getting started."

"I could ask Lucy. She is our maid of all work. I am sure she would be thrilled to have the opportunity to go to London." Lynette paused, and then asked hesitantly, "Would you like to stay to supper, Lord Clitheroe?"

"I think I had better not, Miss Richmond, although I would enjoy the company. I want to arrange for transportation tonight, if possible."

They managed to get through the rest of tea without further embarrassment. James filled her in on the gossip of the last few days, and she discussed the best route to London. Promising to return early in the morning, James took his leave.

26

The Richmonds managed to satisfy all the polite inquiries they received after Lynette's departure. Since Lynette's was a delicate and ethereal beauty, it was not difficult for people to believe that such a young woman could easily become exhausted by the mad pace of the Season. Kate refused some invitations for afternoon drives in order to "keep her sister company," and occasionally one of the family stayed home in the evening, ostensibly for the same reason.

Kate felt very restless, knowing that Lord Clitheroe was on his way to Yorkshire, or already there, and wondering whether Lynette would receive him and if she would return. She was not as great a reader as her father and sister, but one afternoon after three turns around the garden and an unsatisfactory search through her aunt's library for something light to read, she summoned her abigail and set out for Hatchard's.

The booksellers was not very crowded, for she had set out at a time when the *ton* was more likely to be headed for the park than Piccadilly, and she was relieved not to have to answer any more questions about her sister's health.

She had picked up the latest novel from the Minerva Press and was completely engrossed in it when she gradually became aware of a familiar masculine voice making inquiries of a sales clerk. She glanced up and saw that it was indeed Sidmouth. Unfortunately he looked over at her at the same time, and their eyes locked for one moment before she dropped hers to her book in embarrassment. She willed him to finish his business quickly and leave, and tried to interest herself again in the story, but a moment later she sensed his approach.

"Are you going to give me the cut direct, Miss Kate?" he asked ironically.

Kate was forced to raise her eyes from the book. "I must confess that a part of me would like to, Lord Sidmouth, but I would not want to cause any more gossip about the Richmond sisters than has already occurred," she responded coolly.

"I hope your sister is well, Miss Kate. I have heard that she was worn out by the pace of the last few weeks," he continued politely.

"Yes, the activities of the Season are rather tiring. I myself have been glad of the opportunity to stay home at times and keep her company."

"May I inquire when you think it may be possible to call on Miss Richmond? I have never had the opportunity to offer my apology to her."

"We hope by next week she will be recovered, although whether Lynnie will receive you is another matter entirely."

Harry was furious that Miss Kate Richmond obviously was determined to see him in the worst light.

"Miss Kate, as I told you before, my behavior a few nights ago arose from a mistaken reading of your sister's response. And after all, your sister is not completely naive when it comes to . . . ah . . . sensual matters."

Kate was furious. "Are you suggesting—"

"Lower your voice, Miss Kate. We are attracting attention."

Kate continued in a fierce whisper. "Are you suggesting that Lynette is in the habit of enjoying a man's embrace?"

"Not at all. I am merely reminding you that Miss Richmond is quite open and frank about the areas of her research, which would lead one to believe that she would not react to male attention like a frightened girl. I do not think it all my fault for misreading her."

"But I thought you were an expert in these matters," said Kate, with sarcastic sweetness. "Surely you must have seen that Lynnie's frankness had to do only with such matters between the covers of a book."

"I am truly sorry that my own desire blinded me to Miss Richmond's lack of it, but I will not consent to being portrayed by you as the complete villain in this."

"Do you know, Lord Sidmouth," said Kate quietly, "I am not at all sure that what you felt for my sister was desire." Kate said the words slowly as though she were discovering what she thought as she spoke them. Yet as she did, she was sure that she was right. "In fact, my lord, I wonder if you are capable of truly desiring a woman. Would that not mean seeing a woman as an individual? From the gossip I have heard about you, and from your behavior with my sister, you do not seem capable of that." Kate had no idea where her insight came from, but irrational as it might be, she knew she was correctly naming something in Sidmouth. He might appear to be an accomplished lover, he may have broken some hearts, but it seemed to her it was not because he was drawn to women, but that he was running away from something in himself. Her anger at him dissolved in an instant. She looked at him and said, "Actually, I have just realized that I feel very sorry for you, my lord." Kate put down the book she was still holding, picked up her reticule, and summoning her abigail, was on her way out the door before Harry could make his reply.

Not that he had one. With a few choice words, Kate Richmond had gone straight to the heart of the matter. She was right. He hadn't really desired Lynette. Or Lady Sidney. Or Miss Durwood. Or even the few whores he had satisfied himself with over the last year. It was as though he had been trying to convince himself that he wanted them. That he could want a woman again, after what he had seen at Badajoz.

Lynette's journey back was far more pleasant than her trip to Yorkshire. A private chaise was more comfortable than the stage, and with Lucy as her companion, she felt much less self-conscious when they stopped for a meal or overnight. And Lord Clitheroe was proving an enjoyable and thoughtful companion.

During the day he rode next to the chaise and so she had privacy. When they stopped to eat, he joined them. After the first stiffly polite conversation they both relaxed with each other. Because he had at last been open with Lynette and received her willingness to consider him as a suitor, James felt at ease with her for the first time. Sharing meals together and commenting on the sights of the day's traveling gave him great pleasure. He found himself opening up to her, telling her about his family and the long Otley tradition of responsibility. He even, without thinking, started to tell her of the beginning of his long friendship with Harry, and then stopped, apologizing for his insensitivity.

"Do go on, Lord Clitheroe. I am not at all upset with Lord Sidmouth and would enjoy hearing how you met him."

James sketched out their meeting at school and their subsequent years at Oxford.

"You seem to complement one another very well," said Lynette with a smile.

"You mean I am the dull dog and Harry the heartbreaker?"

Lynette protested. "That is not what I meant at all. No, Lord Sidmouth seems rather volatile, and there is a steadying quality in you, Lord Clitheroe, that I am sure he needs. As you need to have your sense of duty leavened by a little lightheartedness."

James smiled. "You have analyzed our friendship very well, Miss Richmond."

"Were you upset when Lord Sidmouth purchased his commission?"

"Envious. I wanted one myself, but was convinced by my mother and uncle that I owed it to the title not to risk my life. Otley duty, you understand. Harry, of course, ignored his family's pleas and went off anyway."

"I have a hard time understanding what there is to be envious of. Surely Lord Sidmouth's injuries convinced you of that?"

"Oh, I know that the Peninsula was a nightmare. Or rather, I don't know, but imagine what it must have been from the newspaper accounts and from the little that Harry and his friends say about it."

"My brother rarely speaks of his experiences either." Lynette looked directly at James. "I admire you for staying, Lord Clitheroe. I think it takes as much strength of character to give up what seems to be the more glamorous course of action as it does to rush off into danger."

"Thank you, Miss Richmond." For the first time since Harry had left him behind, James felt absolved of a lingering shame. He had chafed under his mother's demands yet sometimes secretly wondered if he had used them as an excuse. As much as he had been eager to go, he had also been frightened, and had wondered which had kept him home, his fear or his sense of responsibility. Having someone appreciate the struggle meant a lot to him. And, having seen how close Harry had come to dying, had convinced him, that whatever his motivation, as the earl and his father's only son, he had done the right thing.

"But enough of me, Miss Richmond," said James after a short but comfortable silence. "Tell me, what is it about Padstow that your father must be there on May first?"

Lynette gave him one of her rare and delightfully open smiles, which transformed her from a "faerie queen" to a flesh and blood young woman. "It has long been a dream of my father's to be in Cornwall to see the famous 'Obby 'Oss."

" 'Obby 'Oss?"

"Hobby Horse, Lord Clitheroe," Lynette replied with a chuckle. "Padstow is one of the few small villages where traditional May Day festivities are still held. Many villages have May poles, of course, but the Padstow celebration goes back hundreds of years and lasts from May Eve well into the next day."

"And just what is the significance of a hobby horse?" asked James, picturing a child's ride-on toy.

Lynette surprised herself by blushing for the first time when discussing her father's work. "Horses, among other things, are considered symbols of fertility, Lord Clitheroe. The rites of the old religions were often celebrated to promote the fecundity of the land ... and of people. They were originally sacred ceremonies, of course, but now remain in the form of folk celebrations. My father has long been fascinated by what remains long after the ancient religions have been replaced."

"So people gallop around on little hobby horses, then?" asked James, trying to picture what such a celebration would be like.

Lynette laughed out loud, and then covered her mouth, looking, thought James, like a mischievous young girl.

"Oh, no, Lord Clitheroe, not that kind of horse. The 'Oss—or 'Osses, for there are two at Padstow—are made of a huge hoop covered and skirted with black oilskin. Two men carry them around on their shoulders and dance around the village. Everyone turns out for the singing and dancing. I have always wanted to see it myself."

"Then I am glad I convinced you to come back in time, Miss Richmond."

"So am I," she replied softly.

27

They arrived in London late in the morning, and Lynette was greeted ecstatically by her parents, who despite their outer calm, had secretly been very worried about her flight.

"We will hear the whole story later," said her father after a thorough hug in the hallway. "Upstairs with you. You must be tired from your trip." Mr. Richmond turned to James as Lynette shyly thanked him and said good-bye before going upstairs.

"Lord Clitheroe, I am very grateful to you for bringing her back. I assume that means that Lynette is willing to consider your offer?"

"She has agreed to developing our friendship, Mr. Richmond, with the understanding that I wish to eventually make an offer."

"That is a fine beginning, James."

"Did she say anything to you of her reasons for going home?" asked Lady Elizabeth.

"Nothing. And I did not wish to pry, my lady."

"Very wise, lad," said Mr. Richmond. "I hope we will see you tomorrow night at the Herberts'?"

"Yes, sir, I will be there. But do you think it is too soon for your daughter?"

"I hope she feels recovered, for I doubt that the *ton* will accept our story much longer. The gossips will have her dying of the ague or eloping if she doesn't return soon."

Lynette knew she would have to give her parents a full explanation of why she had returned to Yorkshire, but she wasn't looking forward to it. Despite Gabriel's reassurance, she still felt a certain amount of shame and embarrassment.

She came down shortly before tea and found her father and mother and the dowager marchioness in the morning room. As soon as her mother saw her, she got up and enfolded her in a strong hug.

"I am so glad you returned with Lord Clitheroe, my dear. I have been very worried about you."

"I am sorry for running off like that, Mother. But I had to go home. There was someone I needed to talk to."

Lady Elizabeth looked puzzled and Lynette smiled. "Gabriel Crabtree, Mother."

"Gabriel?"

"Yes. Let us sit down. I must tell you why I left, and it will not be easy."

"Do you want me to leave, dear?" asked her Aunt Kate.

"Oh, no, I would like you to stay."

"*Was* it Sidmouth's behavior?" asked her father.

"Yes and no. He only gave me a few kisses on a balcony, after all." Lynette paused, thinking with amazement that she could say that and mean it. All the terror was going from the memory now that she understood where the fear really came from.

"You see, what happened was that when I leaned back against the balcony I had the strangest sensation that I was back in Yorkshire, my back against a stone wall. When I got home, and tried to remember more, I could actually hear Gabriel's voice."

"Gabriel Crabtree never laid a hand on you?" demanded her father.

"No, no, Father. It was Thomas Halloch. And Gabriel came just in time. In fact, he almost killed Halloch."

"And I always thought he disappeared because he had received a better offer from another farmer somewhere," said Lady Elizabeth, wonderingly. "But why didn't you tell us, Lynnie?"

"I was too embarrassed and ashamed," said Lynette in a low voice. "Somehow, I thought it was my fault. That if I hadn't gone adventuring so early that morning or . . . I can't explain . . . " Lynette's voice was shaking and her aunt got up and put her arm around her.

"I think I understand, my dear. There is no need to put yourself through this again."

"Thank you, Aunt Kate. You see, I didn't remember any of it until Lord Sidmouth kissed me. And even then, not all of it until I was speaking to Gabriel."

"But why didn't Gabriel tell us, or at least tell me. I would have had the bastard hounded out of the county," exclaimed Mr. Richmond.

"I made Gabriel promise, Father. I swore him to silence. He wanted to tell you, but seeing how upset I was, he went along with what I wanted. And I doubt Halloch stayed in Yorkshire after Gabriel had a hold of him!"

"Are you truly able to finish up the Season?" asked her father.

"Yes, I think I am. And although I was a little taken aback by his appearance, I am glad Lord Clitheroe spoke to you and glad you sent him after me."

"Are you interested in marrying him, Lynnie?" asked her mother.

"I can't consider that right now, Mother. I never thought I'd want to be married at all. But now I think that that has something to do with what happened years ago. I feel somehow different. More me, if you can understand what I mean. I am not sure I do," she added with a shaky laugh. "But if I don't know whether I want to marry him, I do know I want to get to know him better."

"So you are ready to go to the Herberts' tomorrow?" asked her father.

Lynette smiled. "Yes, Father. The 'week in bed' has done me a world of good."

"What shall we tell Gareth and Kate, my dear?" asked her aunt.

"As much of the truth as you want. I would rather one of you did it, though, for I don't want to keep going over and over it."

"We understand, dear."

                              * * *

By the next day, Kate and Gareth had heard Lynette's story. Both were helplessly furious with Halloch and were also concerned that Lynette had kept the story to herself all those years.

"The truth is," said Mr. Richmond, "that she almost immediately put it out of her memory and only being with Sidmouth brought it back."

At Sidmouth's name, Kate blushed. She had been so sure that he was at fault, even though Lynette had denied it. And now she was hearing that he really had done no more than steal a kiss or two behind balcony doors. She owed him an apology. She wondered if he would be present that night and if she would have the courage to approach him.

28

Sidmouth was at the Herberts' ball, and having arrived early, heard the Richmonds announced. He was distracted from the light flirtation he had going with the bolder of the two Herbert girls and glanced over at the receiving line where he was surprised to see Miss Richmond looking even more beautiful than usual. Miss Herbert saw the direction of his gaze and looked over herself.

"Ah, I see that Miss Richmond has recovered. She is amazingly beautiful, is she not?" Miss Herbert was generous as well as daring, and Harry looked down at her and gave her his first real smile of the evening.

"For those who like ice-blond beauty. I myself very mush appreciate brunettes."

Miss Herbert, whose hair was a pleasing shade of brown, inclined her head at the compliment.

"They are striking up a waltz, Miss Herbert. May I steal it from whomever you have promised it to?"

Miss Herbert could not resist, and let Harry lead her onto the floor.

James arrived shortly after and went straight over to the Richmonds. After a general greeting, he asked Lynette if she had recovered from her journey.

"I have, Lord Clitheroe, and am very surprised to find myself happy to be back in London."

"May I have a waltz with you this evening, Miss Richmond?"

"I had saved one for you, in hopes that you would ask," she answered shyly.

They chatted comfortably for a few minutes, and Kate watched them out of the corner of her eye. Lynette was more relaxed with Lord Clitheroe than she had seen her with anyone. Kate smiled to herself. It may well be, she thought, that Lynnie would change her mind about marriage by the end of the Season.

Kate turned and saw Sidmouth on the dance floor with Miss Herbert. He was a graceful dancer, and, she had to admit to herself, very handsome in black evening clothes. When the dance ended, she watched him escort his partner off the floor. There was a slight hesitation in his step, which made her realize she had forgotten his injured knee because he danced so easily. She wondered if she would find the opportunity to offer her apology. After the way she had ripped up at him at Hatchard's, he would probably never come near her again.

The slight hesitation in his walk was all that Harry allowed himself. He had been so determined to get his leg back to normal that he had made himself dance, as soon as he was able to give up the walking stick. He found that if he rationed his dances, he could partner a lady as well as he used to as long as he was willing to pay the price of a more pronounced limp by the end of the evening and for part of the next day.

He had decided that he could not ignore Miss Richmond. He did not wish to upset her further, but at the same time, wished to talk with her and reassure himself that he wasn't the reason for her absence. He decided he would ask her to sit out one dance with him in plain sight of her parents, hoping that would feel safe enough to her.

When he approached her, he was surprised to be greeted with more warmth than he would have expected.

"My knee needs a rest, Miss Richmond. I was wondering if you would sit out this dance with me?"

Lynette nodded and Harry guided her over to two chairs a little removed from those set aside for the chaperons. He cleared his throat and was about to begin his apology when

Miss Richmond surprised him again by saying, "I owe you an explanation, Lord Sidmouth."

"Not at all," he protested. "I have heard through both James and your sister that my behavior upset you greatly. I am the one who should explain. I assure you that it is not my way to force myself on a woman. I truly thought you were enjoying my kisses."

"I did not say anything to the contrary, Lord Sidmouth. And remembering back, I can understand your mistake. I cannot give you a full explanation," Lynette continued, after a slight hesitation, "but it was not you that I ran from, but a memory of something unpleasant that had happened to me when I was younger. My reaction was as much to the memory as to your behavior. But I have to add, Lord Sidmouth, that although you are a very handsome and charming man, I did not then and do not now have any strong desire to be kissed by you!"

"How lowering to my self-esteem, Miss Richmond, but, no doubt a healthy blow to my egotism," Harry replied with a grin.

"Oh, dear, that did not come out quite the way I meant it. You *are* very attractive, but it is just I do not respond to you that way myself."

"Stop, Miss Richmond. You have wounded my *amour-propre* quite enough."

"I don't think there is a good way to explain what I mean, my lord."

"You did very well, Miss Richmond! Shall we agree to be acquaintances again, and perhaps even friends? You need have no worry that I will repeat my behavior."

"I would like that very much," Lynette replied.

Kate, who was in conversation with Lord Heronwood and Arden, had been looking over at Sidmouth and Lynette from time to time. She told herself it was because she wanted to be sure her sister was not being made uncomfortable, but she knew that part of what drew her attention was Sidmouth himself. He looked very earnest at first, and then amused. Her sister seemed perfectly comfortable with the situation and Kate made herself concentrate on the conversation going on around her. After a few minutes she had become genuinely involved and did not even notice Sidmouth's approach until he was greeting her companions.

After offering his own opinion on the new production of *Othello*, Sidmouth turned to Kate and requested the next dance.

She studied her dance card intently, as though it were a document of the utmost importance, but as hard as she looked, she could find no one signed up for the next waltz.

"Are you free, Miss Kate?"

"Yes, I suppose I am," replied Kate. She had, after all, wanted to apologize, but had not envisioned doing so with his arms around her. Her lack of polite enthusiasm raised a few eyebrows around her, and she suddenly blushed, realizing how offensive she sounded. "I am sorry, Lord Sidmouth. I was distracted. I would be delighted to dance with you."

After they had been on the dance floor for a few measures, Sidmouth said, without preamble, "That is one of the things I most like about you, Miss Kate Richmond."

"I beg your pardon?" said Kate, looking up into his face and quickly looking down to avoid his teasing eyes.

"Your plain speaking. No polite fictions for you. No, you are honest and practical, like the good Yorkshire lass you are."

"I was at a loss, my lord. After our last meeting, I did not expect you to speak to me again, much less ask me to dance."

"Indeed?"

"You must admit, I was too frank with my opinion of you. And perhaps," she added on a softer note, "a little harsh. I am very protective where Lynette is concerned."

"So I have noticed. But if I assure you I have apologized to your sister and she has accepted my apology, will you relax your guard?"

"Lynette has told us all that happened, and we now know that you are not to blame for her feeling threatened. I have no further fears about you, my lord, and in fact, had intended to offer my own apology for not believing you."

"Good," said Harry. "Then let us enjoy the rest of this dance," he added, pulling her a little bit closer. The pressure of his fingers against her back and the ease with which he whirled her around the room and the intent look on his face all combined to make Kate realize for the first time how easy it might be to succumb to Sidmouth's charm, even if one were determined not to.

After their dance he bowed and thanked her, and left to join a group of his friends, leaving Kate both glad that he had not asked for another dance and disappointed for the same reason.

29

The next morning James called at Harry's just as he was coming downstairs, dressed for riding.

"May I join you, Harry?"

"Of course, James, you are always welcome."

James noticed that his friend's limp was a bit more pronounced than usual as they walked down the front steps.

"Is your knee troubling you again, Harry?"

"It just stiffens up after an evening of dancing, James."

"Should you be riding, then?"

"Yes, James, I should be riding and dancing," observed Harry with exaggerated patience.

"No need to get up in the boughs, Harry. I just worry about you sometimes."

Harry took a deep breath. "I know, James. You are a good friend. It is just that I want to ignore it myself. I am in no real pain, I assure you."

They mounted and made their way through the early morning traffic to the park.

"How about letting them out, James? I need to blow some cobwebs out of my head."

James, who was usually a quieter rider, grinned, and kicking his gelding, was off before Harry could signal his own.

"Oho, if that's the way you want it," he called.

Harry's bay was part Arabian, and he caught up with James and passed him easily. He pulled up under a huge old beech tree and turned and waited.

"You are both too heavy, James," he teased.

"That may be so, but you would never beat us on the hunting field."

"You are right," Harry admitted. "Your gray is a magnificent jumper, while Cinnabar is best on the flat. You seem in good spirits," he added, as they walked their horses to cool them out.

"I am. Mr. Richmond approved my suit and Miss Richmond is willing at least to consider the possibility at some time in the future."

"Congratulations, James."

"You are sure you don't mind?"

"Not at all. I suspect that I saw Miss Richmond as more of a challenge than as a possible fiancée, James. I wish you all the best. I *do* envy you, though."

"How so?"

"Because you so obviously love her. I am just beginning to realize that I may be incapable of any strong feelings for a woman."

"I don't believe that," protested James. "You have seemed driven this year, I admit. But I know you, Harry. You are capable of great love and devotion."

"Perhaps only in friendship, James. Perhaps not with women."

Harry was very happy when James spied Lord and Lady Thorne riding toward them, accompanied by Miss Kate Richmond. He had no desire to continue such a conversation, because the topic only depressed him. He let his friend ride forward and make their hellos and then joined the group himself.

"Does Miss Richmond not ride?" he heard James ask her brother.

"She does, but usually later in the afternoon, and not every day. She is a very competent, but not wildly enthusiastic rider."

"And are you the enthusiastic one, Miss Kate?" Sidmouth asked.

"I am fond of all sorts of exercise including riding, Lord Sidmouth. And I miss the opportunity for a good gallop now and then. Lynette is perfectly content with an easy canter."

"Have you been to Richmond yet, Miss Kate?" James asked.

"Why no, we have not, Lord Clitheroe, although it would seem apropos for a family named Richmond," she said with a smile.

"We must organize a picnic, Harry," exclaimed James, turning to his friend. "Lord and Lady Thorne must join us of course, and the Richmonds. What do you say?"

Harry could hardly refuse, given James's enthusiasm, although, because of the company, he would likely be paired with Kate. They might be on better terms now, but there was something about Kate Richmond that disturbed him. Perhaps it was that she had only seen him at his worst: the violent soldier and the heartless charmer. She knew him a little too well, and he didn't like it.

The Thornes agreed it was a lovely idea, and it was decided that they would go in two days' time.

"For Lynnie and Father will be preparing for their trip to Padstow," explained Gareth.

"What about the rest of the family?" inquired James.

"Mother and I have not decided yet," Kate told him. "But I admit, I am tempted for I have never been to Cornwall and hear it is very beautiful."

"You are very quiet, Harry," observed James as they rode home. "I hope you do not mind my springing that picnic on you?"

"No, James. You need time with Miss Richmond, after all, to succeed in your courtship."

"Yes, and if she is going to Cornwall, I won't be seeing her for over a week."

"I am very sympathetic, James," said Harry with mock seriousness.

"Oh, go on, Harry! And ask Mrs. Brownlee to pack some of her Dundee cake for us."

"Mrs. Brownlee! This picnic was your idea, James. Why should my cook be doing the work?"

"I know, but Mrs. Brownlee is far superior to my own chef for this kind of occasion and you know it."

"All right, James, I will wheedle her into it. I shall see you at the Whitfields' musicale?"

"Yes. And Harry . . . "

"Yes, James?"

"Thank you."

"Anything for true love, Jamie." Harry watched his friend ride down the street and smiled to himself. James was a dear fellow, and his open-heartedness was what drew Harry to him. And what made him feel sad and envious sometimes when he was with him, he had to admit. He only wished that he himself were as uncomplicated.

30

The day of the picnic was clear and quite warm, and all were glad that they had decided to leave early and make it more of a country picnic and not leave it to a more fashionable hour. Harry had ordered his carriage to hold the hampers of food, and he informed the ladies that if any one of them felt the heat, she could take refuge in it.

Although they proceeded out of London in no particular order, with riders adjusting position according to traffic, by the time they were out of the city, they were paired up just as Harry had foreseen. He and Kate were in front, with James and Lynette behind them, and the Thornes bringing up the rear. As good chaperons should, he thought, smiling to himself.

Kate felt a little uncomfortable. She should have foreseen she would be spending time with Sidmouth while James made progress with Lynette, and now that she was riding with him, she had nothing to say. She stole a few quick glances and had to admit that he appeared as well on a horse as he did on the dance floor. He was very handsome, with his black hair and tanned face. Different in build from her father and brother, who were a bit short and very solid. Lord Sidmouth was slim, although certainly not lacking in muscles, she thought, as she saw the way his thighs filled out his buckskins. And his hands . . . Kate shook her head as though to clear it. Whatever was she doing, enumerating all his "points!"

"You are very quiet, Miss Kate."

"I was admiring the beauty of the day, Lord Sidmouth. It is delightful to get out of the city."

"Yes, after Yorkshire, the city feels even dirtier and more crowded. Do you miss Sedbusk?"

"Yes, but not as much as I feared. The Season has been quite pleasant."

"And has it been productive?"

"I am not sure what you mean, my lord."

"You have gathered your own group of admirers around you, Miss Kate. Does any one of them look like he will come up to scratch?"

"That is a rather vulgar question, my lord."

"Merely realistic, my dear Miss Kate. After all, that is what the whole rigmarole is about."

"Then I shall turn it on you. Have you fixed your interest on anyone yet, my lord? You told us in Yorkshire that you were aware of your duty to your title."

"Touché, Miss Kate. Oh, by next year I will undoubtedly have found someone to suit me."

"Was your interest in my sister at all genuine, or was I right about that?" Kate's tone had shifted from teasing to quietly earnest. "Would you have thought of offering for her if she had been attracted to you?"

Harry looked sideways at Kate, who was fooling around with her reins and avoiding his eyes.

"No, I admit that you were right. I had no real feeling for your sister, not as James does. It was her beauty and that aura of remoteness that attracted me."

"And the other young ladies, my lord?"

"I felt less desire for them than for your sister."

"Is there real pleasure in that kind of pursuit, Lord Sidmouth? Truly, I am not trying to insult you. I am just very curious."

"A very unladylike curiosity, I might add," said Harry tartly. "But since we seem to be committed to frankness, yes, there is a certain kind of pleasure in the chase itself, Miss Kate."

Kate blushed. "How will you decide upon a wife, my lord? Will it be the young woman who demands the most determined pursuit, or one who throws herself at you?"

"I haven't given it as much thought as you seem to, Miss

Kate. I suppose I will make my choice based on the usual criteria, given my title and position. I rather think my heart-breaking days are over, anyway. The incident with your sister cured me of that, anyway," admitted Harry.

"I am glad I do not *have* to marry," said Kate thoughtfully. "I never thought I'd be grateful for my family's eccentricities, but because we are so far away from society, I can lead a happy and useful life in Yorkshire. You, on the other hand, because of your title, *must* marry. It is odd, but in this particular situation, as a woman, I have a little more freedom."

"Are you sure you would be happy living out your days on a Yorkshire sheep farm, Miss Kate? Particularly if your sister marries, and you are the only one at home with your parents?"

"It is such an odd idea to me, Lynnie getting married," said Kate, sidestepping his question. "Do you think she would be happy if she accepted Lord Clitheroe?"

"James is a good, solid man and will make an excellent husband. And I think, despite their differences in temperament, or perhaps because of them, they could be very happy together."

Kate looked ahead and watched James and Lynette chatting comfortably with one another. Her sister was more at ease with Lord Clitheroe than with any man she'd encountered.

"You may well be right, Lord Sidmouth. I hope you are."

When they reached Richmond, Harry had his coachman and groom set up the picnic in the shade of a huge oak tree. They were all delighted to be out of the sun, and Harry had lemonade served before the food was completely set out. And when they did sit down to eat, there was not a lot of conversation, for they were all hungry after the ride.

"Harry, please thank Mrs. Brownlee for her efforts," said James, brandishing a chicken leg.

"Save some room, James, for the Dundee cake."

"Strawberry tarts and Dundee cake," said Lady Arden. "I will never be able to climb back on my horse."

"We will have plenty of time to rest or take slow, digestive walks, my dear," replied her husband with a grin.

After a few minutes of relaxation, James got them moving. "If we don't walk, I will disgrace myself by nodding off right here," he announced. And so they formed a walking party, this time with Kate and Sidmouth in front and James and Lynette bringing up the rear.

The path was wide and well-tended, and it was therefore a complete surprise to Harry when his boot caught in a protruding tree root, pitching him forward. He kept himself from falling only by putting all his weight on his bad leg.

"Bloody hell," he muttered, as he felt the knee protest.

"Are you all right, my lord?" Kate asked solicitously.

"Yes," he answered through clenched teeth. "Damnation . . . I am sorry, Miss Kate, I can't seem to keep from swearing."

"Don't worry, I have heard worse from our shepherds," she said with a grin. "Is your knee all right?"

"Oh, yes, I suppose so," Harry replied, flexing it with a grimace. "It will just be a little stiffer tomorrow, that's all."

"Can you walk on it?"

Harry took a few steps. "Yes, it is fine, Miss Kate. I am sorry to make such a fuss. I just get furious when I realize I don't have the mobility I used to have."

"Perhaps we should turn around? We seem to be far ahead of the others anyway."

They turned and started back slowly. Kate noticed that Sidmouth was limping and wondered if he was in pain and not admitting it.

"Why don't you take my arm, my lord," she offered. "It would take some of the weight off your leg."

Harry was not in great pain, as a matter of fact. The limp was more from stiffness than anything, but he decided he would take Miss Kate Richmond's arm anyway.

"Does that feel better, my lord?"

"Much, thank you."

Kate found herself feeling a bit warm, and she did not think it was the sun. It was disconcerting to have Sidmouth so close. It was also strange to have him in need of her assistance. He didn't strike her as a man who enjoyed being dependent on anyone for anything, particularly a woman.

Harry was very conscious of Kate's arm beneath his. He kept his weight off his knee as much as he could and found himself responding to the combined slenderness and strength of her arm. She wore a light flower scent that he had not noticed before. He realized he had not noticed a lot about Miss Kate Richmond, glancing over at her profile. He had never noticed, for instance, the way her brown curls clustered around her face. Or the length of her eyelashes. He realized he didn't even remember what color her eyes were.

"I am not too much of a burden, Miss Kate?"

"Not at all, my lord," said Kate, looking up to reassure him.

Gray. Her eyes were gray. A steady, clear gray, with a slight hint of blue.

Kate immediately looked down to avoid Harry's gaze.

"Does your knee still hurt, my lord?"

"Hardly at all, Miss Kate."

Both were so absorbed in their response to one another's closeness that they were almost upon Gareth and Arden before they were aware of it.

Gareth fumed when he saw his sister's arm in Sidmouth's. Then he realized it was Sidmouth's arm on hers, and that the marquess was limping.

"Are you all right, Sidmouth?"

Harry removed his arm from Kate's and took a step on his own. "Yes, quite. I stumbled back there and landed all the weight on my bad knee. Your sister was kind enough to offer her support." He turned to Kate. "Thank you, my dear. I am all right on my own now."

Gareth stepped in between the marquess and his sister, and they continued back down the path. When they caught up with James and Lynette, Gareth almost laughed out loud, for Lynette's arm was drawn through James's, and they were walking back to the picnic site, oblivious to the others. Gareth stepped over to his wife and muttered, "I am a terrible chaperon, Arden. Both my sisters arm in arm with a man!"

"That is because you were paying too much attention to me, Gareth. Stealing kisses instead of watching your sisters!" she teased.

"Next time we bring Aunt Kate," he declared.

31

When they reached the picnic site, they found everything packed and back in the coach.

"There is room inside for two of the ladies, my lord,"
Harry's groom informed him.

None of the ladies was interested, however, and so they
set off. This time, Gareth made sure he was next to Kate,
while Arden's companion was Lord Sidmouth.

When they reached the Thorne town house, James realized that the family would be on their way to Cornwall the
day after tomorrow and that he would not be seeing Lynette
again for well over a week. He said his good-byes and wondered how he would survive the next ten days.

"Harry, where are you off to now?" he asked.

"Home to change, James."

"May I come back with you for a drink?"

"Of course," replied his friend, wondering what was in
James's mind. It was not like him to go visiting before
changing out of dusty riding clothes. He guessed it must
have something to do with Miss Richmond.

He was right. As soon as they reached the house, Harry
ushered James into the library and asked him what was on
his mind.

"I have no feeling of progress in my courtship of Miss
Richmond," he replied.

"But there you were today, walking arm in arm with her,
James. Surely she wouldn't allow that if she didn't take you
seriously?"

"Oh, I think she is beginning to see me as a friend. But I
don't feel a . . . physical response from her, if you know

what I mean, Harry. And I am afraid to attempt a kiss after your fiasco."

"Perhaps Miss Richmond is not capable of a physical response, James. Have you thought of that? Although it would be a shame, wouldn't it," Harry continued almost to himself, "for that amazing beauty to go to waste."

"She is not a cold woman, Harry, I am sure."

"No, I didn't mean that. There are some women who are just more interested in affection than in sensuality, James. Would you still want to marry her if that were so?"

"I think so. You see, I love her very much. And there is something about her that makes me want to protect her," James answered. "Do you suppose her lack of response has to do with me, Harry? I have not had the success with women you have had. Maybe I just don't inspire her to passion?"

"Don't be so envious of my so-called success, Jamie! Of course, with the right woman, you will spark passion. I am wondering if you have been too careful with Miss Richmond? You need more time with her."

"And I am losing more than a week as it is . . . "

"Have you ever been to Cornwall, James?"

"Why, yes, years ago."

"Well, why not go again. In fact, we could travel down together, if you like. I confess to some curiosity about this May Day festival. And Miss Richmond would be impressed with your interest in her scholarship."

James's face lit up. "That is a splendid idea. I can't believe I never thought of it myself. Are you sure you won't be bored, Harry? I really will appreciate your company. I would feel I was intruding upon the family, otherwise."

"Don't be so grateful, James. I am rather bored with the usual round, and the Richmonds are the most interesting family I have met in a long time." Harry did not add that he would also be happy to see more of Miss Kate Richmond, for he was not at all sure why that should be so. "Now go off and start packing or do something useful with yourself. I want to get into a hot bath and soak my damned knee."

A half hour later, as he lay soaking in his bath, Harry

found himself thinking about the Richmond sisters. It was very odd, he realized, that much as he had wanted, nay needed to break through Miss Richmond's remoteness, he had, her sister was right, no real desire for her. Oh, his pulse had raced at the thought of her perfect face and silver gilt hair. And he had wanted to kiss her. But he had not realized until now, thinking back to that night, that he had not wanted *her*.

Yet now, lying in scented hot water, feeling all the tension and stiffness drain out of him, he found himself drifting back to the picnic and the sensation of leaning upon Kate Richmond's arm and gazing down into her honest gray eyes. He could close his eyes and see her, and the sensations that aroused were quite different from what he had felt for any woman since he returned home from the army. He was not feeling compelled to pursue Kate Richmond or to force her to respond to him. Instead, he was drifting in a sort of liquid state and felt more open and relaxed than he had in months. In fact, he felt desire for the first time in a long while, for as he lay there, her image floating in and out of his mind, he could feel himself growing hard merely at the thought of dropping a gentle kiss on top of her head— or tipping her chin back and touching her lips with his . . .

"Oh, God," he groaned, "I had better call for cold water!" He stood up suddenly and grabbing the bowl of clean water by the side of the tub, poured it over himself. It was by no means cold enough, but it was cooler than his bath and his fantasies, and did the trick.

He was glad, he thought, as he toweled himself dry, that he had suggested the trip to Cornwall. It would give him time to further his acquaintance with Miss Kate Richmond.

32

All the Richmonds, including the dowager marchioness, had decided to make the journey to Padstow. Gareth offered the Thorne coach for the trip and declared that he would ride alongside so that they wouldn't need two vehicles. He regretted it by the end of their first day on the road. The weather, which had been glorious for the last week or so, changed two hours after they left the city. The temperature dropped, and a fine rain began to fall, so that by the time they reached the first inn, Gareth was cold and damp. The next morning the rain was no longer a drizzle but a downpour. His family protested that they could squeeze him into the coach, but he insisted on riding and was soaked after fifteen minutes. He had not been so uncomfortable since his Peninsula days and was in a foul mood by the time they stopped for the night. When Arden fussed over him, he snapped at her. Another woman might have been silenced, but not Arden, who snapped back that she had indeed married a rudesby. "There is no reason to take out your temper on me, Gareth. After all, you could have been warm and dry inside the coach."

"And made you all most uncomfortable. I knew I shouldn't have come. This has become like my worst memories of the trips we took in my childhood, bad weather and bad tempers."

"Yours is the only bad temper so far, Gareth," his wife remarked and left him there, half-dressed, and went to join the others in the private parlor.

The next day it rained even harder, if that were possible, and Gareth gave in and squeezed beside his wife. The coach was roomy, but not made for seven, so by the time they stopped for tea, Gareth's was not the only temper that was frayed. The trip was tedious, the roads rutted, the coach overcrowded, and all but Lynette and Mr. Richmond were wondering why on earth they had decided to come. If it had not been raining so hard, they would at least have been able to enjoy and comment on the scenery, but as it was, they could see nothing.

Thank God, thought Kate, as she drank her tea, we have only a half day's journey to go. I don't think I can stand any more. She was certainly not alone in her thoughts, for the rest were counting the hours, too.

Lynette had passed some of the time trying to picture what the 'oss would really look like. It was one thing to read about it and see drawings; it would be quite another to experience it. She was surprised, however, that her thoughts kept wandering away from Cornwall and to London and Lord Clitheroe. She was beginning to like him very much. Perhaps "like" was too mild a term. She had great affection for him. He was kind and generous and thoughtful and had not pressured her at all. Beyond walking arm in arm at the picnic, he had barely touched her. Why had he hardly touched her? she wondered. Sidmouth had taken every opportunity even before the balcony fiasco, whereas James had done nothing very much at all beyond holding her a little close while dancing. And now she realized, she was beginning to want him to. He was very handsome in his own way. Very solid. She wondered what it would be like to rest her head on his shoulder. She thought it would be very nice. She wondered what it would be like to kiss him. Her mind would shy away from the image, but not in sheer panic, as with Lord Sidmouth. There was still a part of her that was scared, but more of her seemed to be curious, and yes, even desirous.

If the Richmonds' journey was uncomfortable, it was nothing compared to James's and Harry's. They had decided to ride, since it would be faster, but after the first day of rain, James insisted on renting a chaise. Unfortunately the chaise was not at all well-sprung, and they suffered even more than the Richmonds from the bad roads. They were a half day behind and never met the other party at any of the inns along the way. Harry, in fact, was convinced that they were the only fools on the road. "The Richmonds probably turned back long ago," he complained. "We will be the only outsiders there watching this ridiculous horse, whatever it is—if they hold the damn ritual in the rain, which they probably do not!"

James, who had had more than enough of Harry's ill-temper, almost threw a plate of stew at him. "Stuff it, Harry. This was your bloody idea, so you'd bloody well better enjoy yourself." It was so unlike James that Harry looked at him in amazement, and then struck by the awfulness of their journey, could only laugh. This set James off, and their helpless laughter restored both of them to good temper.

33

The two men arrived in Padstow late in the afternoon of April thirtieth, May Eve. It was still raining, although not as hard, and was beginning to look as though it might clear up by evening.

Padstow was a small fishing village with a crescent-shaped harbor and steep streets rising up from the beach. It looked like any other little fishing town in Cornwall, and as James and Harry looked around, they marveled that this particular town, out of all the others on the coast, had kept an ancient ritual alive.

There was a maypole in the town square that was in the process of being decorated, despite the rain. Across the narrow streets were strung lines from which hung all the flags of the town's small fleet. The gaiety and color of the displays began to lift James's and Harry's spirits, despite the weather—until they sought for accommodations. There was no real inn in the village, only the Golden Lion pub. When they questioned the pubkeeper about rooms, he looked at them with amusement.

"I do be having a room at the top of the stairs there," he said and pointed, "but you'll get no sleep here tonight."

"We don't mind a little noise, do we, James?" said Harry. "We'll take it."

The pubkeeper smiled broadly, pocketing Harry's money and showing him up the stairs. "Now, don't say I didn't warn you."

The room was small, with two cots that took up most of the space. "But it is a damned sight better to stretch out and sleep than to be jounced around in that chaise," said Harry as he lay down on one of the cots.

"I am going to look around, Harry. I'll be back to get you before supper."

"Looking for the Richmonds, eh? Good luck to you, James."

James went down to the bar and asked for a pint of ale. As the barkeep was pulling it for him, James questioned him about the celebration.

"How long has this been going on?"

"Well, some say two or three thousand years," said the barkeep. "But I can't swear to that, of course. I can tell you that my grandfather and his grandfather and *his* grandfather all remembered it."

"Do many people come and watch?"

"All of us from Padstow, of course. Even those that have moved away. They always come back, just for May Day. And there are always some folk from other towns and even from London, like yourself."

"Are there others down here from the city?"

"There be a few, I've heard. Mrs. Couts has taken in a whole family. I hear the gentleman is a scholar and wants to study the 'oss."

"Ah, that must be my friends the Richmonds," said James. "They must have gotten the last accommodation."

"Yes, but they booked ahead, I believe."

"Very smart of them," said James, finishing the last of his ale. "I think I will explore the town a little."

"It won't take you long, sir, as it's a little town," joked the barkeep. "But at least it has stopped raining."

James was relieved to find that this was so. He walked down to the quay, where the found the tide out and the boats drawn up in a semicircle. The sky was getting lighter, despite the hour, and the late afternoon sun at last broke through, lighting up the streets and striking all the windows of the town so they shown gold. It was a moment a painter would have relished, thought James, for the combination of light and shadow was breathtaking. His spirits lifted, and he felt, despite the hardships of the journey, that it had been the right thing to do. He only hoped Harry would think so.

The Richmonds had settled in comfortably at Mrs. Couts, having arrived earlier in the day. She had been recommended to Mr. Richmond by an old friend as someone who took in paying guests, and she was a delightful hostess and marvelous cook. The younger people had explored the town before tea, in spite of the rain and were content to sit in front of a warm fire and play whist for a few hours.

"Now, I want all of you in bed early," said Mr. Richmond, as though he were speaking to a group of ten-year-olds.

Gareth looked up and grinned. "But Father, we want to stay up late tonight."

His father laughed. "Oh, I suppose I did sound ridiculous. All I meant was that you don't want to miss a minute of tomorrow morning."

"And what are you planning to do tonight, Edward?" asked his wife.

"I am not going to bed at all, my dear. I shall be down at the Golden Lion watching them dance. I understand that some of the best dancing takes place before the actual celebration. And maybe I'll also have a chance to get some of my questions answered."

"And, of course, only men are allowed in the pub," remarked his wife.

"I am afraid so, my dear."

"Perhaps I'll go down with you," said Gareth.

Lynette looked over at her father and said, "It seems most unfair that Gareth can just walk in, and I, who am more interested cannot go at all!"

Aunt Kate looked up from her cards. "I heartily agree with you, child. Is there nothing you can do about it, Edward?"

"There is no one here who knows us," commented Lady Elizabeth. "And Lynette is tall and slim enough for a lad . . ."

"What are you suggesting, Elizabeth?" asked her husband.

"I am suggesting that you and Gareth rummage through your clothes and find something suitable now, so that we can make any alterations that are necessary right away."

"You can't mean to let her dress up as a boy, Elizabeth?"

"Oh, why not, Father. I'll be very quiet and just stay in the background. If I put my hair up under a cap, no one will ever guess."

"Well, I understand your eagerness, Lynnie. And it is unfair that after all your scholarship, you don't get to do a little field work."

"I'll be there to watch out for her, Father," said Gareth.

"All right, all right, I give in. Go upstairs, Gareth, and see what shirts and pants you can come up with."

Of course they almost gave up the whole scheme when Lynette first tried on her brother's shirt and pants. "Our heights are not that different, Gareth, but our widths . . . "

"Never mind," said her aunt, through a mouthful of pins. "We'll manage. We have a few hours yet."

Somehow they did manage. They tucked and pinned and hemmed and finally put together something that fit. Not very fashionably, but at least Lynette no longer had to hold her pants up with her hands.

"We can't do anything with the jacket, though, Gareth," said his mother.

"Mrs. Couts's stable lad looked about Lynnie's size," said Kate.

Gareth went out and came back with a navy blue wool jacket.

"I had to buy it, and he thought me very strange to be paying good money for something that won't fit me, but here it is. And his cap, too."

It fit almost perfectly. And when Lynette tucked her hair up, she looked enough like a boy to get by, as long as she was quiet and stayed by her father and brother.

The three of them left at around ten. Lynette felt as excited as she had when she went pretending as a child. To her this was more exciting than going to any London soiree, and she swaggered along between her father and brother, feeling freer than she had in years.

The pub was crowded and the tables had been pushed back to clear space in the middle. There were two old men with accordions and three drummers, and shortly after the Richmonds' arrival, the music began. It was clear that the musicians were just warming up, for the barkeep was still serving rounds of ale. Lynette was looking delightedly around her when she saw two men come down the back stairs and grasped her brother's arm.

"Gareth, isn't that Lord Sidmouth and Lord Clitheroe? What on earth would they be doing here?"

"Why, so it is! I am sure I don't know. On second thought, maybe I do," replied Gareth, looking soulfully at his sister.

"But James never said anything to me."

"Perhaps he meant to surprise you. I suppose he didn't want to be separated from you for so long."

Lynette was turning hot and then cold. The fact that James had followed her here, had been interested enough in her and her work, was very satisfying. But here she was, disgracefully dressed in man's clothes, in a pub late at night. Whatever would an Otley think!

James and Harry were disoriented for a few minutes. They had retired early and had both awakened at the same time to the sound of the music.

"Oh God, I suppose this is what the landlord meant when he said we wouldn't sleep well," groaned Harry.

They had tried to ignore the noise, but that proved impossible.

"We might as well give up and go down, Harry," said James. "This must be the beginning of the whole celebration," and so they had dressed and made their way down, wondering about the open space in the middle of the pub. They had only time for one ale before the barkeep closed up the bar.

"Look, Harry. Isn't that Thorne? And his father?"

"Yes, so it is. Whatever is going on must have something

to do with the ritual, for Richmond is no late-night carouser, I would wager."

The two men squeezed their way through the crowd and greeted Gareth and his father. They ignored Lynette, or rather, made no connection at first, between them and the slight lad standing nearby.

"What is going on, Mr. Richmond?" asked Harry.

"There is usually some good dancing the night before," he replied.

"Like Morris dancing?"

"I don't think so. The men will be practicing being under the 'oss."

At that moment the drums began a rhythmic tattoo, and people started singing and two young men took the floor.

It was dancing unlike they had ever seen. There was an initial pattern of a prancing step with a waving of arms, and then, when the music changed and got slower, the two young men were down on the floor, approaching and nuzzling one another, as though they were indeed horses. And then the drums would beat faster, and they were up again in the original dance.

It went on and on, and the beat of the drums and repetitive melody and movement were mesmerizing. James, who was standing next to Lynette, felt all the years of being a dutiful Otley melt away, and it was only himself, James, who was standing there. Not the viscount, not the good son, but the original human being he was born to be.

Lynette was equally moved. At first her scholar's mind had been trying to keep mental notes, memorizing the movements, analyzing the words of the song. But after a few minutes she too was one with what was being enacted before her. It seemed to her that the pub disappeared, that all vestiges of civilization were gone, and they were on some hillside watching the original dancers. Without thinking, she reached out for James and whispered, "Isn't it amazing, James?"

Her touch burned right through him. He knew her immediately, and looked down at her face, which was lifted up to his. Her eyes were wide with apprehension as she realized that she'd inadvertently revealed herself. James smiled at the sight of the "faerie queen" dressed as a common village lad. She was real; she was, for the first time, reachable and touchable and without thinking, he leaned down and kissed her lightly on the lips. Lynette felt herself open for him. There was no fear, no memory flashing in front of her eyes. Just James, who was looking at her with both tenderness and passion. She felt released, as though all the energy she had been holding back for years was now hers again. She wanted to dance. She wanted to be out there with James, moving low on the ground and nuzzling each other. She wanted him, and it was such a new and wonderful feeling that she felt like tossing her hair back like a mane and . . .

They were lucky that only Harry and Gareth had seen James's kiss. Harry was momentarily horrified as he saw his friend lean down to kiss a lad on the mouth. He too had been caught up in the dance, but not quite to that extent, and he was about to pull James away when he saw Gareth lean over and whisper in the lad's ear. As the boy stepped back, face burning, Harry realized it was Miss Richmond. Of course, he thought, she would never have been able to keep away from this. But thank God Gareth had separated them before someone else had spotted them. Although, God knew, given the warmth and openness in the pub, and the sensuality of the dance, perhaps no one would have cared.

34

When the clock struck midnight, the focus suddenly shifted from the music inside to the outside of the Golden Lion, where a chorus of villagers had gathered.

"It is the night song," someone shouted, and the door to the pub was flung open so the singers could be heard.

> Rise up, Mr. Brown, we sing the night song in all the town.
> We'll tramp through your garden and march through your lanes
> Our chorus will rattle your window panes,

the townspeople chanted, and then began the song.

> "Rise up, Mrs. Johnson and gold be your ring
> For summer is a comin' today
> And give to us a cup of ale and merrily we will sing
> In this merry morning of May."

After a few choruses aimed at the pubkeeper and his wife, the singers moved on.

The singing went on for hours. By the time the other Richmonds got down to the town square early the next morning, Gareth, his father, Lynette and the others had been around the town and back. Despite their lack of sleep, they were wide-awake and greeted the rest of the family with raucous good cheer, as though they were indeed townsfolk. Kate looked at her sister with amazement. She had never seen Lynette so alive. Her eyes were sparkling, and she was moving so freely in her boy's clothes that Kate quite envied her.

Lady Elizabeth looked at James and Harry with surprise. "How did you get here, my lords?"

Harry laughed. "I expect the same way you did. It was a miserable journey in the rain, but I have decided it was well worth it."

James felt it necessary to give a further explanation. "We were so intrigued by Mr. Richmond's account, that we thought we should not miss this opportunity to—"

"To follow my daughter." Lady Elizabeth completed his sentence with dry humor.

"Oh, well, yes. I came to see Miss Lynette, and I found her and we had an evening . . ."

"Mother, it was an amazing night . . ."

"I can see that, Lynnie, and the ritual hasn't even begun."

"I don't see how the horse can be any better," said Gareth.

Mr. Richmond looked around and waved his arm. The sun was shining, making the drops of rain on the primroses, cowslips, and bluebells on the maypole shine like small diamonds. The flags were snapping in the breeze, and the silver gray leaves of the sycamore boughs that lined the front of the pubs gave the feeling they were in a wood. It did indeed seem like a climactic moment. But just then a great shout went up in front of the pub, like a hip, hip hooray:

> Oss, oss, wee oss
> Oss, oss, wee oss,
> Oss, oss, wee oss.

And around the front came the first of the two horses.

Kate had never seen anything like it. She had seen maypoles and Morris dancers and Midsummer fires. But all those things were very English. But this fantastic creature looked as though it came from another place altogether. A black-tarred cloth was draped over a huge hoop on which was mounted a small mock horse's head. And on top of the horse, from the middle of the hoop, the rider emerged, covered by a tall black mask, with features painted in red and white.

A young man dressed something like a Morris dancer and bearing what appeared to be a short-handled broom, led the horse out into the square. And then they started dancing.

Those who had been in the pub could recognize some of the movements, particularly those of the "teaser," or young man with the club. The horse danced and the hoop swayed and the crowd sang.

> Unite and unite and let us unite
> for summer is a come un today
> And whither we are going we all will unite
> In the merry morning of May.

The drums were beating insistently, the first tattoo that Harry had ever heard that did not have to do with soldiering or killing or dying. They were beating in life, not death. As one of the drummers had explained last night, they were waking up the earth.

They sang "rise up," to the pub owner and his wife again. They wandered slowly through the town, stopping at every window to greet an old woman or man. "Or else the old 'uns would feel left out," explained one of the townsmen next to Harry.

After every three or four verses, a strange thing would happen. The drums would stop, the singing became slower and more plaintive, and the horse would sink down.

The words they sang to this slower melody made absolutely no sense to Harry. But the tune . . . the tune struck a chord, with its sadness. It was almost sadder, in fact, because the words meant nothing.

The teaser slid his club under the 'oss and then the club slid out. The young dancer grabbed his club and thumped the horse, and the horse jumped up, alive again after his short death. Harry felt like leaping up with the horse, too, and yet, when they sang another verse, just before the horse "died" again, he felt grief squeeze his heart for all the companions he had lost.

> Oh where are the young men that now do advance
> For summer is a come un today
> Some they are in England and some they are in
>   France
> In the merry morning of May.

And some, he thought, as the horse sank down again, are bones bleaching in piles under the sun of Portugal and Spain. He felt tears running down his cheeks, and he could not have said if he was crying from grief or from joy, for the two feelings were so intermingled. There was such great joy in the singing and the dancing and the thought of the greenness of spring. It was most certainly a ritual of unity and coming together. There was no thought of rank or privilege, old or young, rich or poor, friend or enemy. And yet every time the chorus was sung, Harry felt that unique human grief for unity lost, for the separations that life inevitably brings.

At one point they stopped in the square again. Three young women from the village were clustered together opposite him, and he noticed that Kate Richmond was next to them, her face flushed with excitement.

"Where are the maidens that here now should sing," sang the villagers while the three girls giggled and hid their faces in their hands.

"They're over in the meadows, the flowers gathering . . . " There was a slight pause, and then the teaser grabbed the nearest girl as she shrieked with delight and thrust her under the skirt of the horse.

"Unite and unite . . . " sang the townspeople while the four feet under the hoop continued to dance. When the chorus was done, the girl emerged, her face covered in soot and all the people gave a great shout of satisfaction. When Harry asked an older woman next to him what it was all about, she told him that if a girl came out smudged with tar, she would be married by Christmas.

Someone, somehow, had gotten Kate's name, for the next verse was sung directly to her.

> Rise up, Miss Kate, all in your gown of silk
> For summer is a come un today
> And all your body yonder as white as any milk
> On the merry morning of May

Kate blushed a deep red and started shaking her head as the teaser approached, but it was no use. She, too, was pushed under the horse and Harry watched her feet shuffle awkwardly until she found the pattern and rhythm of the dance.

When she emerged there was an even louder shout, for not only was her face sooty, but her arms and skirt were smudged with the sticky black tar that covered the horse's skirt.

The dancing went on all day and into the evening. In the late afternoon, Aunt Kate dropped out and retired to the bench in front of the pub where she shared a pint with one of the old-age pensioners and listened to stories about the ritual. But the rest of them, tired as they were, kept going until it was all over.

There were a number of new verses added after the Miss Kate verse, but Harry couldn't sing them. Every time he opened his mouth, all he could think of was "And all your body yonder as white as any milk." At one point the dance brought him next to Kate, and she looked up at him and smiled unself-consciously. All he saw was she in a gown of silk and her body under it. He grew as hard as the maypole for a moment and wanted to pull her out of the crowd and into a private corner where he could love her. He was shaken by the strong surge of desire that swept through him and let the crowd sweep him away before he did something outrageous. He had no difficulty at all believing that the "Wee 'Oss" might lead to a rash of babies exactly nine months after May Day, no matter what happened to the crops.

35

K ate, knowing only the little that her father and Lynette had told them about the ritual, was unprepared for the power of it. It was not a power that manifested itself suddenly and strikingly, like the first sight of those great stones at Stonehenge. It was a gentler, more joyful power, but an insistent one, for all its softness. She felt the same mingling of joy and grief that Sidmouth had. The villagers of Padstow led their routine lives three hundred and sixty-four days of the year and then, on this one, because of their faithfulness to the tradition, they were able to create a space where dying and coming back to life, light and dark, the softness of flowers and the hardness of the maypole were remembered and celebrated.

She had been so caught up in the rhythm of the drums and her amusement at the young woman before her, that she had not realized she was about to be pulled under until it happened. It had been hot and dark under the horse, and being hidden gave her the permission to attempt to join the dance. The tarred skirt had moved up and down, and she could feel it sticking to her arm and leaving a residue. And when she reemerged, she felt freer than she ever had in her life: free of all practical concerns, free of all worries about accounts, and free of civilized constraints. When Harry Lifton suddenly appeared next to her later, she had smiled up at him in good fellowship. And then he looked at her in such a way that made her as hot all over as she had been under the skirt of the 'oss. She realized anew how handsome he was, in a gypsyish way with his black hair and tanned face. He looked as relaxed and free as she felt. Had she been a village girl and he one of the fishermen of Padstow, they would probably have headed off hand in hand to some hidden place to indulge in that rite more ancient than the hobby horse. The thought of lying down with him in green grass, of feeling his lean body hard against hers, made her almost gasp for breath. As the tide of people swept her on, she tried to forget the image of her body and his body entwined together. And how could she even be thinking of such a thing when she wasn't even sure she liked Lord Sidmouth!

When the drums and the dancing finally stopped, it was almost ten at night. The Richmonds, who had been carried along by the energy of the villagers, were suddenly exhausted. The dowager marchioness had made her way back to Mrs. Couts hours ago, and now the rest of the family followed her. James, who had kept close to Lynette the whole day, walked up the hill with them. As they said good-bye at the door, Mr. Richmond, taking pity on James's obvious reluctance to leave, invited him for a late breakfast the next morning. "I am sure Mrs. Couts won't mind setting the table for one more. No, two. Do invite Sidmouth to join us also."

James's face lit up, and he said his good-byes quite happily.

All slept late the next morning, and Mrs. Couts's breakfast was served midday to a very subdued group of travelers.

The two married couples were comfortably silent, but the four younger people were ill-at-ease with one another. James's new-found confidence with Lynette seemed to have deserted him, and he felt as awkward as he had in the beginning of their acquaintance. And Harry, who found himself seated next to Kate, was unable to summon any of his easy charm and confined himself to such brilliant utterances as "Could you pass me the cream, Miss Kate. Thank you."

It was as if all had been lifted up into a world greater

than their own yesterday, and then dropped back down again with a collective thud. There were no words to describe the experience, yet they all tried, realizing immediately how flat their comments were.

Aunt Kate was very aware of the undercurrents at the table and rather amused. Perhaps it was because she had sat out and watched and then gotten some sleep after it all and so didn't feel as much of a letdown. Her sharp eyes had not missed James's kiss nor the fact that Harry Lifton's attention had been fixed on Kate.

She believed that James and Lynette were well on their way to a happy ending. James was perfect for her eldest niece. Despite their shyness this morning, the dowager was sure that when James formally proposed, Lynette would accept.

The more she thought of Sidmouth and Kate together, the more she was convinced they would make a splendid couple. Not that anyone else would come to that conclusion, she thought with amusement as she observed them this morning. But Sidmouth, with his fey charm, was just what the practical Kate needed. There was something that worried her about the marquess, however. His father had also been wild, but Harry underneath his devil-may-care exterior was far more intense than his father, she was sure. There was something eating away at him, and she was afraid that having recklessly cut a swathe through the latest crop of young ladies, he might pick one out at random, marry her, and make both their lives miserable.

She had never played matchmaker in her life, but as she watched Kate and Harry, she decided it was never too late to begin. Her intuition had ensured her survival on the streets of the worst neighborhoods. She decided she would trust it now and do her best to help her niece and Sidmouth to see the possibilities of a future together.

36

The first week they were back in London was disorienting for all of them. They had experienced something timeless and far more real than the superficialities that surrounded them in London. The contrast between artificial politeness and the openness and warmth of Padstow was so great that they almost felt they had reentered an alien world, though it was their own.

Of all of them, James was perhaps the most disoriented. He had lived his life so properly, so dutifully, that he had never questioned anything around him. Otleys were unfailingly polite, properly reserved, married according to money and position, and brought more little Otleys into the world who would continue on the same way. Had he been away like Harry, his view would have been changed. As it was, until their brush with death in Yorkshire, James had never looked at his life from a different perspective. Coming out of the freezing world of the Yorkshire storm and into the warmth of the Richmond family had begun a change in James that culminated with the trip to Padstow. He came home feeling emotionally alive, and for the first time in his life aware of how dead to the world of feeling his family was.

His mother had been increasingly worried about his attention to Miss Richmond and his obstinate refusal to woo either of the two young women the family had picked out for him. His abrupt departure to follow the eccentric Richmonds to Cornwall to view some heathen celebration had driven her to summon her brother-in-law the bishop, and on his third day back James was summoned into the library by his mother and uncle.

"James," his mother declared, "your uncle has something he wishes to speak with you about. I will leave you alone for a few moments."

As Lady Otley got up to leave, James motioned her to remain. "I think you should stay, Mother," he said mildly, but with the implied expectation that she would heed him. Lady Otley sank back down on the sofa, surprised at her son and herself. It was the first time he had assumed an air of command since his father died.

"Now, what do you have to say to me, Uncle Herbert?" James was sure he knew, but was willing to play the scene out.

"Your mother summoned me because of her grave concern regarding the health of your soul."

"My soul?"

"She informs me that you went haring off to Cornwall to take part in some . . . pagan rite."

"I suppose it might be considered that," James admitted. "It is, after all, a celebration that predates Christianity. But what that has to do with the health of my soul, I am sure I don't know."

"I knew Edward Richmond at Oxford. He is, at the very least, an eccentric agnostic. I cannot think that a friendship with that family to be at all healthy for you."

"For an Otley, you mean?"

"Yes, James. And being an Otley is nothing to sneer at," said his mother.

"I am not sneering, Mother. But I am afraid I am a bit weary of always being an Otley first and myself afterward."

"The Otleys have always been a God-fearing, respectable family. And great privilege carries great responsibilities, James," the bishop intoned as though speaking from a pulpit.

"That may be true, but being an Otley is also not much fun," replied James with a twinkle in his eye.

"Fun! Of course not. Life is a serious business, and life as the Viscount Clitheroe very serious indeed."

"But do my duty to name and title mean giving up all duty to myself?"

"James, what has yourself got to do with anything?" demanded his uncle. "It is that ridiculous preoccupation with self that has led to scandals like Lord Byron and Caro Lamb. It is all very well for self-styled poets and madwomen to ignore society and family, but never for an Otley."

"We are wondering, James," his mother asked, "whom you have chosen for your viscountess, Miss Hargraves or Miss Clement?"

"Neither," James replied.

"You see, Brother, I was afraid of this!" exclaimed Lady Clitheroe.

"What do you mean, neither, James?" asked the bishop coldly.

A year ago, James would have been utterly intimidated by his uncle's tone and his mother's form of emotional blackmail. But today he realized he was free of all the Otley prating about duty and responsibility.

"I intend to make Miss Lynette Richmond my viscountess. If I can persuade her to marry me, that is."

His mother gasped. "I knew it. It is Harry Sidmouth that is responsible for all this. I have never understood your friendship with such a rakeshame. But he has managed to turn you against your family at last."

"Don't be ridiculous, Mother," James snapped, losing patience at last. "I have followed your rules all my life. I have always done what *you* wanted. I am a grown man and it is time to do what I want. And I want Miss Lynette Richmond."

"But they are a very odd family, to put it in the mildest of terms, James," protested his uncle. "They never come down for the Season. They are not at all religious. And Lady Elizabeth, as if the scandal of elopement wasn't enough, has taken to sheep breeding."

"And has made a great success of it," replied James stoutly.

"Do you know what her sister-in-law does, James?" demanded his mother. "Why she is called the Methodist marchioness?"

"Some charitable work in the poorer areas of the city, I believe. I have met her, and she is a delightful woman."

"Charitable work! You tell him, Brother. I am feeling ill and must go and lie down."

James led his mother to the door and summoned a maid to help her upstairs.

"The dowager marchioness spends her time giving out hygienic information to women of the streets, James. Now do you see why an Otley could never marry into such a family. She encourages prostitution."

"Don't you think rather it is poverty that encourages prostitution, Uncle? One can hardly hold Lady Tremayne responsible?"

"It would be one thing if she were out there trying to save these unfortunates. But she does nothing but help them avoid disease."

"That is no small thing, Uncle." To tell the truth, James *was* a bit shocked by the bishop's revelation and was doing his thinking aloud. The more he thought about it, however, the more sensible it seemed. "Surely true piety includes a genuine care for the body as well as the soul?"

"I can see it is useless to argue with you, James. Are you truly set on this course?"

"I love Miss Richmond very much. I think she will be very good for me and I for her. I have lived the first part of my life according to what Otleys do. I intend to live the rest of it according to what this particular Otley wants to do."

"Then I can only pray for you, Nephew."

"I will appreciate your prayers, your grace," replied James with a smile. "And now I must take my leave. I have promised my company to Lord Sidmouth this morning."

It was a lovely day, and James decided to walk to Harry's. Taking a stand against his uncle and mother, declaring his independence, made him feel light and free and when he was ushered into Harry's morning room, his friend immediately noticed the difference.

"You are obviously over the top about something, James. Did you propose and Miss Richmond accept?"

"Not yet, Harry," James replied with a big smile.

"Then what has you looking so happy?"

"This morning I feel like I can do anything I want to do," said James, seating himself at Harry's table and beginning to butter a slice of toast.

"And why is that?" Harry was both delighted and intrigued by the new James.

"Because I have stood up to my uncle and mother at last!"

"What! Defied the Otleys? I can't believe it."

"Believe it, Harry. My mother summoned my uncle supposedly to minister to the health of my soul. But in reality, they both wished to make sure I did not disgrace the Otley name by furthering my acquaintance with the Richmond family."

"And you told them . . . ?"

"That I intend to make Miss Richmond my viscountess if she will have me."

"Well done, James!"

"I never realized before how stuffy and preachy Uncle Herbert is. But I suppose one doesn't get to be a bishop any other way! I wonder what kind of clergyman Edward Richmond would have made?"

"A poor one, I would guess."

James laughed. "I suppose you are right. He is too honest and independent to toady to the Church hierarchy. And his sister-in-law's activities would have kept him from a lucrative living if nothing else did. Do you know what she does, Harry?"

"The Methodist Marchioness? Yes, I thought everyone did."

"I knew she worked directly with the poor, and I've even heard of her infamous bodyguard. But that she advises prostitutes on hygienic matters . . ."

"A little too much for your Otley sensibilities, James?" teased Harry.

James blushed. "Well, I was a little shocked. But then, when I began to think about it, it seems far less hypocritical than condemning them and leaving them in poverty."

"I have to agree. And at least hypocritical is not a word one would use about the Richmond family. But when are you going to ask Miss Richmond for her hand, James?"

"I would like to wait a bit longer. Well, that is not precisely true. I would like to ask her today! But I want to be sure that our kiss was not just due to the magical atmosphere of Padstow."

37

Had he but known it, Miss Richmond had thought of little else but James Otley, Lord Clitheroe, and his kiss. She too wondered if it had occurred only because of the moment, or whether James would attempt another. He had declared his intention to court her, but Lynette had never had any man persist in his courtship once he got over being dazzled by her beauty. She had so little experience that she felt like a sixteen-year-old, shaken by her first infatuation. She had awakened one morning from a delightfully disturbing dream of James kissing her, and walked through the day in a daze, most of her wanting to be back in her dream.

The evening of the Langley rout her hands were trembling as she tied her cloak. She knew that James would be there, that he would ask her to dance, and the thought of being held in his arms shook her to the core.

When she entered the ballroom, James was immediately at her side. He thought she had never looked more beautiful. Her gown was embroidered with silver thread and seed pearls, and she had pearls woven in through her hair. But tonight there was something about her beauty that invited him closer. He signed himself up for two waltzes, one of which was a supper dance.

During their first waltz, Lynette was unable to look into James's face. She would lift her eyes briefly and respond to a question and then drop them again.

"You seem to find my lapel fascinating, Miss Richmond," James teased gently.

Lynette blushed. "I am afraid I am still embarrassed by my behavior at Padstow."

James wasn't sure if the oblique reference to their kiss was a good or bad sign.

"Was it only embarrassment that you felt, Miss Richmond?"

"Oh, no," Lynette replied softly.

"Then you might be persuaded to repeat the experience?"

"Yes," she responded, bravely looking right into James's eyes.

James watched her face flush pink and pulled her a little closer to him as he said, "It is a very warm evening, Miss Richmond. Perhaps we could walk in the garden after this dance."

Other couples had had the same idea, but James and Lynette managed to find a little privacy by the herb garden, where they sat on a small stone bench. The scent of mint and thyme perfumed the air.

"Our first kiss was in rather unusual circumstances, Miss Richmond. I would like to be sure that a second is what you want. I would not like to hurry you."

Lynette looked up and saw the look of both longing and concern in James's eyes. She had accepted that James cared for her because he had told her so, but it had remained more of an intellectual acceptance. But she had not really felt it before. Now she did. He did not only want her, but he also loved her. She let herself open to the sensation of being loved. Their first kiss had come more on her part, from a sense of joy and fellowship than desire. But tonight she was suddenly flooded with it. She slid closer and lifted her face up to his, a clear invitation. James leaned down and brushed her lips lightly. They were both taken aback that such a brief contact struck strong sparks. Without thinking Lynette put her arms around James's neck and pulled him into a deeper kiss. When he finally pulled back, they were both breathless.

James heard footsteps and soft laughter and realized that some other couple was making their way down the path to the herb garden.

"We had better go, my love," he said, the endearment

slipping out as he reached out to brush back a strand of her hair.

Lynette nodded and slipped her hand into his without thinking. James linked his fingers through hers and thought he had never been so happy. The approaching couple was too preoccupied to notice them, and so he kept hold of Lynette's hand until they reached the doors leading back into the ballroom. He returned her to her family, nodded politely, and said coolly that he was looking forward to their next dance.

When he returned for his waltz later in the evening, Lynette went straight into his arms. Neither spoke. Neither had to. They were silent with each other at supper, although they chatted politely to the others around them.

At the end of the evening James bade Lynette good night, adding quietly, "I would like to take you for a drive tomorrow morning, Miss Richmond?" She nodded her consent, knowing that tomorrow would formalize what had been decided between them tonight.

Lord Sidmouth had confined himself that evening to dancing with respectable widows and matrons. There was no singling out of one young woman, no laughing pursuit to make her feel the center of his attention. The only unmarried women he danced with were the Misses Richmond. It was well known that Lord Clitheroe was obviously after the elder sister. It was also known that Miss Kate had never shown any particular interest in Lord Sidmouth, and this evening did nothing to dispel that impression. She accepted his invitation politely, they smiled and chatted on the dance floor, and he bowed politely and returned her to her brother's company.

In fact Harry felt quite a stranger to himself. He had spent the better part of a year pursuing young women he had no real interest in. He had become expert in arousing expectations without compromising himself. And now that he had discovered an interest in Miss Kate Richmond, it was as though he had forgotten everything he knew about flirtation and courtship. He wasn't feeling driven, but drawn slowly and inexorably to her. And he discovered a diffidence he had not known he possessed.

Kate was also puzzled by his behavior and her own reaction to it. She had despised him for his easy charm, and had been furious at his behavior with Lynette. She had forgiven him that, of course, when the truth came out, but had still seen him as careless and had vowed she would not be taken in.

The way he had looked at her in Cornwall when their paths had crossed and their eyes met during that long day of singing and dancing almost undid her resolve. And tonight, when he asked her to dance (and she was well aware she was the only unmarried female aside from her sister he had partnered), she had armed herself against this charm. But it was rather like preparing for a battle that never occurred. He was polite, he held her at exactly the proper distance, and he wasn't charming at all. She wondered why he had even bothered to ask her since he treated her like an aging spinster who held no attractions for a man.

She was annoyed with both herself and him for the rest of the evening. With him for not being his more easily dismissable lightweight, and with herself for having wanted him to be. Just so she could have given him his comeuppance, of course. But was she so unattractive to him that he didn't even care to try?

She was in a very bad mood indeed by the end of the evening. She hated her ambivalence, and yet she was probably the only young woman in London he had not tried to maneuver onto a balcony or out into the garden. She despised his rakish behavior and yet wanted him to act the rake with her!

Her night was long and fretful, her sleep interrupted by dreams of Sidmouth. In one, she was walking down a garden path, and at every turning she came upon the marquess with yet another woman on his arm. In another, she was living on an unrealistically long street in Mayfair, and emerged from her door only to see other young ladies emerging from theirs and stretching out their arms to accept beautiful floral tributes all being delivered by Lord Sidmouth's footman, while she stood empty-handed.

Harry's evening was not much better. The ball had been very tame, nay, boring, except for his one dance with Kate. But then that dance had probably bored *her* to tears, for he had been about as exciting a partner as Bishop Otley!

When he got home, he also tossed and turned, finally giving up on sleep and going down to his library to pour himself a brandy. The May Day song from Padstow kept running through his head, and he kept seeing Kate's face as she was dragged laughing and protesting under the 'oss. It was such a strong, honest, open face. Not plain, but certainly not beautiful. Kate Richmond was a young woman of integrity, common sense, and a sense of humor. She had not been afraid to confront him about his supposed behavior with her sister. He had certainly been mildly aware of her as a woman before Cornwall, but now there was nothing but that awareness. It drew him to her side like a lodestone, and at the same time it paralyzed him once he was there. Surely it was ironic that the one woman he finally thought he was capable of loving made him lose everything he needed to woo her: his charm, his intensity and most of all, his unavailability. For he knew it was that challenge that drew women the most. They often wanted men desperately whom they knew they could never have. The present irony was that Miss Kate Richmond could have him, all of him, and most likely would therefore never want him.

38

James arrived to take Lynette for the promised drive in the late morning. He wished to avoid the later crowds and hoped they would be able to find a secluded corner of the park. Lynette had her abigail with her, but he had already primed his groom to distract the young woman long enough for him to have some time alone with Miss Richmond.

When they reached the park, he was relieved to see it was fairly deserted. The early morning had been sunny, but the day had grown increasingly cloudy, and that had probably kept people away. Of course, going for a walk when it was threatening rain was not the most romantic idea, but he had his groom drive them to a certain spot he knew where a path led into the trees on the edge of the park. "Henry, Miss Richmond and I are going to stretch our legs. After you have secured the horses, please escort her abigail and join us."

Henry winked at Lynette's maid. " 'E wants a little time alone with your mistress, luv. Shall we give it to 'im?"

"My mistress already told me to give them fifteen minutes. But no more."

"Wot! Miss Richmond said that?"

"Oh, no, not Miss Richmond. The dowager marchioness is really my mistress, and she thinks Lord Clitheroe is going to propose today."

"Well, 'e tipped me this for nothing then." Henry grinned, pulling a guinea out of his pocket. "But I won't tell if you won't."

* * *

James glanced back once or twice, but there was no one following yet, so he assumed his scheme had worked. He drew Lynette's arm through his and felt her tremble a little.

"You are not worried about being alone with me, I trust?"

"No, James, I am not."

It took him a minute to realize she had used his first name. "You called me James."

Lynette started to apologize, saying it had just slipped out.

"Please don't apologize, my dear. Just give me permission to call you Lynette."

"Yes, James, I should like that."

They were walking slowly, arm in arm, each thrilled by the unaccustomed intimacy of the secluded path, their physical closeness, and their mutual desire to be more to each other than Miss Richmond and Lord Clitheroe, when James heard a soft pattering. At first he thought it was someone following. Then he realized it was raindrops falling on the leaves over their heads.

"Damn," he said aloud.

"What is it, James?" asked his surprised companion.

"It is starting to rain."

Lynette put out her hand and a few raindrops hit it. "I believe it is."

"We will have to turn around."

"So soon?"

"I cannot let you get wet, my dear."

"You forget I am a Yorkshire lass," she said with a mischievous smile. "T'weather doesn't bother me."

James stopped and turned toward her. "I had imagined a warm day with the sun dappling the path," he said with a rueful smile. "There is a small clearing ahead where I might have spread out my coat and knelt at your feet . . ."

Lynette laughed. "Then I am glad it is raining, James, for I could never have that."

"You do know that I love you?"

"It would be nice to hear you say it," she answered shyly.

"I love you, Miss Lynette Richmond." James had clasped her hands in his and was looking intently into her face. "And it *is* you I love, Lynette, and not just your beauty. Is there any hope that you might come to love me?"

"No hope, I am afraid, James."

The look in his eyes was so awful that Lynette immediately regretted her teasing.

"No hope, James," she continued quickly, "because I already love you."

James forgot all propriety in his relief and crushed her against him, raining kisses on her face and neck that made them both forget the rain itself, which was beginning to come down harder and faster.

It was only when James felt her gown beginning to get wet that he pulled back. "We'll have to return to the carriage, I'm afraid," he said, pulling off his coat and placing it over her shoulders.

"One more kiss," whispered Lynette, who was too hungry for his mouth on hers to let him go so soon. And so James bent down once again and was surprised to feel her lips opening over his, inviting him to make the kiss deeper.

"I think it is good that it is raining," said James when he finally pulled away.

Lynette blushed, and they turned back down the path, this time with James's arm over her shoulders and his arm around her waist. Before they reached the carriage, however, Lynette stopped and looked up at him. "James. Didn't you forget something?"

James looked around. "Why, no, I don't think there is anything we left behind."

"Didn't you mean to ask me to marry you, Lord Clitheroe?"

"Why, I did, didn't I?"

"No, you didn't, James," Lynette replied, her eyes laughing up at him.

James started to sputter an apology.

"Yes, James, I will marry you, if you will only ask me."

"Will you indeed, Miss Richmond?" James asked, smiling at his own confusion and her teasing.

"I will, Lord Clitheroe."

The ride home was anticlimactic. Because of the abigail's presence, there was no opportunity for anything more than brushing hands. When they reached the house, however, the maid slipped out quickly and Henry took a long time with the horses, which gave James a minute or two to engage his fianceé in another passionate kiss.

When he finally broke away, he asked if her father was home. "For although I already have his permission, we should tell him our news."

"He is most likely in the library, working on his book."

"Oh, dear," groaned James.

"What is it, James?"

"I am feeling very foolish, but I have completely forgotten about your research."

"Are you bothered by it, James? As a member of the eccentric Richmond family, I have been free to do what I want. Will I have to change if I become an Otley?" Lynette held her breath. She loved him, but she was not about to give up that part of her life.

"I am afraid your duties as viscountess will pull you away from your work more than you would wish. Do you think you can stand that?"

"Do you wish to live completely immersed in Society, James?" she countered.

"To tell you the truth, no. We will, of course, have to spend some time in London, but we can use my estate in Yorkshire to get away from everyone."

"And the Otleys will not mind a bluestocking daughter-in-law?"

"The Otleys," declared James, "will do what I tell them, as head of the family."

Lynette giggled.

"I sound pompous, don't I?"

"Only a little. But seriously, James, have you considered what marriage into my family means for you? The gossips will have a field day."

"I love you, Lynette Richmond, and your family could be a team of Morris dancers, for all I care."

"Father *has* danced with the men of Bainbridge, James. I am sure he would teach you," she replied with mock seriousness.

James laughed. "Enough of your teasing, woman. Let us get inside and make our announcement."

39

The Richmonds' response to the news was, of course, far different from the Otleys. Her father looked long and hard into his daughter's eyes and then gave her a long hug, which helped him mask his emotion. He was quite satisfied with the clear-eyed happiness shining from Lynette's face. Lady Elizabeth, once she had offered her congratulations, drew James aside and started talking to him about his plans for the Yorkshire estate.

"Be careful, James," cautioned her husband, "or Elizabeth will have you running more sheep than you have room for."

"I am hoping that Lynette and I can spend quite a bit of time there, so I welcome any ideas for improvement," James replied.

Kate had a hard time controlling her emotions. The look on James and Lynette's faces brought tears to her eyes. Her sister, whom no one had ever thought would marry, was clearly head over heels in love with Lord Clitheroe. But Lynette's marriage, no matter how much time she spent in Yorkshire, meant that Kate would be very much alone. First Gareth gone, and now Lynette. And so I will be the unwed sister, taking care of our parents and the household, she thought. She was ashamed that the tears in her eyes were both from happiness and the thought of her own loneliness. As she watched Lynette and James, she couldn't help wondering what it would have been like to be the one announcing a betrothal to Lord Sidmouth. Lord Sidmouth, indeed, she immediately scolded herself. The man had barely said two words to her over the last few days, much less expressed any particular interest.

The dowager marchioness was very much aware of what her younger niece must be feeling. The Season would soon come to an end, and Kate would return to Richmond House, nothing in her life changed. She was determined to speak with her niece alone and requested her company on a shopping expedition the next day. Kate was surprised, because her aunt was far more likely to be off doing her work than traipsing in and out of shops looking at silks and ribbons. But she was pleased to be asked and happy to know she would be away from what was sure to be almost constant chatter about the coming wedding. Despite Lady Elizabeth and Lynette's usual lack of interest in the usual female pursuits, mother and daughter seemed almost immediately consumed by planning the first wedding in the family all would be present for.

After an hour of shopping, during which Aunt Kate purchased her niece a new reticule and bought a bit of antique lace for Lynette's gown, the dowager complained that she was tired and hungry and suggested that they stop at Gunter's for a cup of tea. After they were served, Kate looked over at her aunt and grinned. The dowager was licking cream from a pastry, just like a cat licking up milk.

"I do believe this whole trip was just an excuse for you to have one of these confections, Aunt Kate!"

Her aunt dabbed at her lips and smiled. "I do confess that stopping for tea has always been my favorite part of shopping. But I did have another reason."

"Yes?"

"I wanted a chance to speak with you alone, my dear. I am wondering how you are feeling about all the excitement surrounding your sister's betrothal."

"I am delighted for Lynette, as you know, Aunt."

"Of course. We all are. But in my happiness for Lynette, I haven't forgotten you will be returning home with your parents, while Lynette will be starting her married life. Are you very disappointed you haven't received an offer?"

Kate sighed. "Very disappointed would be too strong,

Aunt Kate. But I do have some qualms about being the spinster daughter. Especially, I am ashamed to confess, since we all assumed that Lynette would be the one who remained at home and continued her work with Father. I thought I was more likely to be married."

"Is there no one for whom you feel a preference?"

Kate hesitated before she replied. "I have had strong feelings about only one man, Aunt. But when I say strong feelings, I do not mean all positive," she added, with a low, trembling laugh. "The Marquess of Sidmouth has provoked me to anger, annoyance, fear, and, I must also confess, attraction."

"Fear?" replied her aunt with surprise.

"There was a disturbing occurrence early on in our acquaintance. I realize that it was a result of his experiences on the Peninsula, for I do not think he is a truly violent man." Kate told her aunt the story of the picnic. "And, in addition to whatever he is carrying about with him as a result of the war, he is a terrible rake!"

"Yes, so it seems from the outside. Has he tried his charm on you?"

"No," replied Kate. "To my great relief . . . and disappointment."

They both laughed. "Ah, yes," said the dowager, "it is one thing to disapprove of a rake. Quite another to feel slighted by him. Yet I am not sure that Lord Sidmouth *is* a confirmed rake."

"He has confined himself to married ladies since we returned from Cornwall," Kate admitted.

"He has also danced with you and Lynette, I believe?"

"Yes, but he has hardly said two words to me. In fact, I am almost ready to believe that his charm was only an illusion."

"But do you, nevertheless, find him attractive?"

"Yes," replied Kate slowly. "Although I am ashamed to confess it."

"Why ashamed, my dear? He is a very attractive man. If I were younger . . ."

"But surely one would wish to be attracted where there is

a mutual respect and interest? He is clearly not interested in me. And I am not at all sure how much I respect him. Although, I must confess, I did, from the beginning, misjudge him about Lynnie. But he disturbs me, Aunt Kate, in a way no man ever has."

"Good," declared the dowager.

"Good?"

"Yes, I am glad to see the very practical Miss Kate Richmond is not always practical and rational. And I think you and the marquess would be very well suited."

"Aunt Kate!"

"Oh, I have been keeping my eye on the two of you. I think it is a good sign, in fact, that he is treating you differently from those other young ladies he was pursuing."

"Most likely he knows it is because James was wooing Lynette. They are very good friends and obviously we will be seeing him from time to time."

"That could be. But I noticed how he looked at you in Padstow."

Kate blushed.

"But you are right. There is something under the surface. Not for you to be afraid of, I am sure, my dear. My intuition about people rarely fails me. The Marquess of Sidmouth is not a violent man. He has, however, some demon that has been driving him. The question is, can that demon be exorcised?"

"I think your charitable work is quite enough for you, Aunt Kate. You do not need to take on the exorcism of demons," declared Kate, and she changed the topic of conversation to lighter matters.

40

When Miss Richmond's betrothal was announced, there was the usual gossip, made spicier because she was marrying into the Otley family, and everyone knew that the Otleys had chosen someone else for the viscount. James's mother, despite her disapproval, was nothing if not loyal to her own son, and refused to be drawn into any criticism, however veiled, of her future in-laws, and managed to survive quite well a family dinner with the Richmonds.

The wedding was to take place in Yorkshire at the end of August. James naturally had asked Harry to stand up for him, so his friend was often invited to the Otleys or the Richmonds for what, he told James, were negotiations worthy of a Wellington campaign.

Lady Otley wanted her son married in a large, society wedding. Lynette wanted to be married in the Hawes parish church, with a simple wedding breakfast at Richmond House. James insisted that since it was her wedding, she could have whatever she wanted. But compromise was reached along the way. Lady Otley would have her chance to shine as a hostess by offering a pre-wedding rout at the end of the Season to which she would invite everyone who was anyone.

Harry enjoyed watching James come into his own. No, the Bishop would not marry them, for the family had a warm relationship with the vicar at Hawes. But he would be most welcome, James added, to baptize their first child. Harry nearly laughed aloud at the expression on Lady Otley's face at that one.

As he watched James and Lynette together, he wondered

that he had ever wanted those kisses on the balcony. She was one of the most beautiful women he had ever met, but he no longer desired her beauty. Again and again he felt pulled to Kate Richmond's side, only to find himself acting like a raw, inexperienced youth, unable to think of any but the most obvious comments on the wedding or the weather.

As he felt himself drawn closer into the Richmond family circle, he found himself most comfortable with the dowager marchioness. She shared his amusement at the Otley-Richmond maneuvers. He was able to talk naturally to her and enjoyed her witty observations on society in general and the Otleys in particular.

One evening, at the interval of a musical evening which they both attended, he wandered over to where she was standing alone.

"You have been deserted, Lady Tremayne?"

"Not at all. My nephew and his wife are around somewhere, getting me some refreshment."

"May I keep you company until they return? Such a handsome woman should not be standing alone."

"You are a very charming man, Lord Sidmouth. You remind me of your father."

"Ah, yes, I had forgotten you knew him."

"Indeed, had your mother not arrived upon the scene, I would have been quite tempted to pursue him. Not, of course, that he would have responded to pursuit. I suspect you are very like him in that respect."

Sidmouth lifted his eyebrows. "I confess to a desire to run in the other direction if a pushing mama with her daughter in tow comes my way."

"And a tendency to pursue those young ladies whose mamas wish to keep you away?"

Harry gave a mock flinch. "A direct hit, Lady Tremayne."

"Although I have noticed that your behavior has changed over the past weeks."

"Indeed?"

"Oh, do not take that haughty tone with me, young man.

Old women like me have plenty of time to observe. And I have been worried about you."

"About me?" Harry hid his immediate reaction, but was touched to think that the dowager actually cared about him. "There is nothing for you to worry about."

"I have a soft spot in my heart for the son of old friends. And so I worry, my lord. But I can see that I have put your back up, and as I have a favor to ask you, I will pursue it no further."

"I am yours to command, my lady," replied Harry with a deep bow and a flourish of his hand, wanting to return the conversation to a more superficial level.

"I need an escort tomorrow."

"To the opera? Is the family not going? I would be happy to take you."

"No, I need someone tomorrow afternoon. My usual bodyguard has the toothache, and cannot accompany me. But perhaps you would prefer not to? I could ask Gareth if you have other plans."

"I said I was yours to command, Lady Tremayne. What time do you need me?"

"Two o'clock?"

"I will see you then."

When Harry awoke the next morning and remembered what he had committed himself to, he groaned. The last place in the world he wished to go was St. Giles. Yet he could hardly let the dowager go alone. He liked her very much, admired her, and was also amused by her eccentricity.

After a light nuncheon, he changed his clothes, having decided that buckskins and a Belcher handkerchief were less likely to draw attention than a Weston coat and trone d'amour. When he arrived at the Richmonds, Lady Tremayne was waiting and nodded her approval.

"Very wise, Lord Sidmouth. They will know you are a gentleman, of course, but at least your clothes don't flaunt it."

Lord Sidmouth's coachman dropped them off in St.

Giles and promised to return in a few hours. As they walked down the street, a few street peddlers nodded to them and the dowager smiled back, greeting them by name.

"However did you get started doing this?" asked Harry.

"One evening after the theater, my husband and I were accosted by a young prostitute carrying a baby. It was obvious that both mother and child had been infected by the pox. It shocked and appalled and shamed me, that I should be so happy and well off and that a woman not much younger than I was slowly rotting away. I had heard Wesley preach when I was young and had been much affected. It seemed that there was a chance to put some of my so-called Christian beliefs into practice."

"I imagine some people would think that handing out the information you do is hardly Christian."

"Then they have not read their testaments. Christ had great sympathy for whores. Look at Mary Magdalene."

"But he did say 'Go and sin no more.' "

"But then I am not Christ, Lord Sidmouth. Who am I to say that to anyone when I am well-clothed and well-fed. I would rather tell the so-called gentlemen who frequent these streets to go and sin no more!"

"I hadn't thought of it from that perspective," Harry admitted.

They had come to a dark, dank tenement that listed on its foundation. Three dirty children were playing outside, and Sidmouth was sure he saw a rat scurrying inside to escape the stalking of an emaciated cat, which one of the children sought to pick up. The cat slunk off before Harry could step in and protect the child from the animal most likely infected with God-knew-what diseases.

"I am going to visit someone in this building. You may wait outside, if you wish."

"Of course not," said Harry stoutly, although the last thing he wanted to do was to enter the building. He followed the dowager upstairs. The house was airless and the stench abominable. In a small room on the third floor they found a young girl of about fourteen lying on a dirty pallet. Her face was discolored with old bruises and her arm strapped to her side, but her eyes lit up when she saw Lady Tremayne.

"How are you feeling today, Betty?"

"Much better, my lady."

"I have brought you some food, which I will leave here. And I have instructed the doctor to visit you again tomorrow. Is there anything else I can do?"

"No, ma'am. You have already been too good to me . . ."

"Do you remember the name and address I gave you?"

"Yes. Mrs. Blisse Spencer."

"She runs a clean, safe house, Betty. She makes sure that her girls are not roughly treated. And she will help you to protect yourself from disease and conception. I will stop in on her in a week or so. I hope I will see you there?"

"You will, my lady, you will."

41

They left and visited two more houses where the dowager was known and welcomed. One of them was almost out of St. Giles, on the edge of a better neighborhood. The house was whitewashed, and there were none of the ever-present rats. They were admitted by a cheeky young Cockney girl who joked with Lady Tremayne about her escort. "Are you bringin' us customers now, my lady?"

"Lord Sidmouth is just helping me out today, Mattie. Is Mrs. Spencer available?"

"Yes, mum. I'll go get 'er."

They were shown into a private parlor that was tastefully if inexpensively furnished. Harry was greatly surprised to see a reproduction of a Constable on the wall. He would not have thought a brothel owner to have such good taste.

"I am sure you are surprised to see that here," said the woman who entered, as if she had read his mind.

"Indeed I am. It is a good copy."

"It is not a copy, sir. It is a parting gift from a former protector."

Harry's eyebrows lifted in surprise. "Then you could get a bit of money for it, I should think."

"I could. But its sentimental value is far more important to me."

Mrs. Spencer, for it was she, turned and greeted the dowager warmly. "Do you have time for a cup of tea today?"

"I am sorry, Blisse. I have only come to remind you of Betty."

"Ah, yes. The young girl who met up with a rough customer. When shall I expect her?"

"In a few days. But may I leave her address? In case she doesn't come on her own, could you send someone over for her?"

Harry was fascinated by the easy familiarity with which the two women conversed, the short, gray-haired marchioness and the proprietress of a brothel. "Mrs." Spencer was tall, raven-haired (obviously not a natural color), and hard-eyed. She did not look at all like the sort who would keep valuable paintings for sentimental reasons, nor take in young girls for safekeeping. She looked like what she was, a businesswoman in a heartless profession. And yet, there was something about her mouth that belied the expression in her eyes. It was full and soft and curved. To his amazement, Harry found himself wondering what it would be like to kiss her. Somehow, a woman who possessed a tender mouth like that must still possess some tender feelings.

Mrs. Spencer escorted them to the door herself and offered her hand to Lady Tremayne, who held it and thanked her again for Betty. When they were back out on the street, Harry looked down at the dowager and smiled.

"You are quite a woman, Lady Tremayne."

"Given the privilege I grew up with, Mrs. Spencer is more to be admired, Lord Sidmouth. She has managed to keep her humanity in a very hard world. Were you disturbed by what you saw today, my lord?"

"I saw nothing I didn't know existed, although I admit it is different to experience it rather than hear about it. But nothing that was worse than the war."

"Yes, I had forgotten about that. We at home can never really guess at what it must have been like."

"I confess to being disturbed by the sight of that first young woman," Harry said slowly, his throat getting tight. "She reminded me of something that I saw at Badajoz. It scares me, such violence," said Harry, looking directly at the dowager. "Because it comes out of what is supposed to be an act of love. Or at least desire."

"And do you fear desire, my lord?" the dowager asked softly.

"I believe I do. I am beginning to see that my pursuit of young women had little to do with real desire, which your niece was wise enough to see."

"My niece?"

"Yes. Miss Kate Richmond and I had an enlightening conversation after my disastrous behavior with her sister," Harry admitted with a tight smile.

"I am not at all sure your behavior was disastrous, my lord. Oh, I would not recommend consistently letting your own needs blind you to those of young women," the dowager continued, answering Harry's look of surprise. "But your behavior on that balcony brought back an important memory for Lynette. She was attacked as a child, you see, and not only had buried the incident, but all her ability to feel passionately. Had you not kissed her, she might have remained unable to open herself to love. Life is paradoxical, isn't it, Lord Sidmouth," said the dowager. "And not all meetings between women and men are characterized by violence. You have been exposed to the extremes, and I understand your fear of opening your heart. But that does not mean you do not have one."

"Would that I could believe that, Lady Tremayne," replied Harry, who took her arm and silently escorted her to where the carriage was waiting.

42

Kate had been very surprised by her aunt's decision to use Lord Sidmouth as an escort. She was also a little hurt. Surely she could have accompanied her aunt if Absolution was unavailable.

When the dowager returned, Kate was waiting for her.

"How was your afternoon, Aunt Kate?"

"Very productive, thank you." Lady Tremayne smiled to herself. Her work was very taken for granted by the family, and no one ever waited around to inquire about a particular afternoon. She was sure it was curiosity about her companion that motivated her niece.

"Is Absolution sick, Aunt Kate? Will you need someone later in the week? I would be pleased to accompany you."

"Absolution is fine, my dear. But I thank you for your offer."

"Then why did you use Lord Sidmouth, Aunt? And how did you get him to come?"

"I told him that Absolution was laid low by the toothache."

"And he is not? And you lied to Lord Sidmouth to get him to go with you?" said Kate, surprised at her aunt's deception.

The dowager had the grace to look a little ashamed of herself. "Well, it was the only way I could think of to spend some time with him alone. I wanted to get to know him better."

"And why is that, Aunt Kate?"

"Because, as I have told you, I think you and he are well-matched. But something has been standing in his way. And now I think I have an idea of what it is."

"Most likely it is that he is not at all interested in me!" Kate responded tartly.

"No, I think it is that he is afraid."

"Afraid? Afraid of what?"

"Afraid of himself. Something happened at Badajoz, even beyond the expected horrors of a battle, I am sure. It is amazing to me that we continue to send our young men off to war, where violence is everyday, and then expect them to return home untouched. I suspect that Lord Sidmouth was marked as much emotionally as physically by his experiences."

Kate spent the rest of the afternoon thinking about Lord Sidmouth. What could he have done or seen that might have affected him so, if her aunt was right? His behavior had been different since their return from Cornwall. Might he really be interested in her but somehow afraid of that interest? But what was there in plain Kate Richmond to attract or frighten him?

Her own feelings puzzled her just as much. She had initially found Lord Sidmouth easy to despise. At the same time she had been mildly attracted to him. The mild attraction had grown much stronger over the course of their acquaintance. What would she feel if she knew her interest was returned? She was very much afraid that she wanted to feel the strength in those hands again, this time restrained by tenderness—to feel him stroke her cheek, to feel his lips on hers.

But had that anything to do with love? Or was it only desire?

Perhaps it was because she had spent all afternoon thinking of him, but when she saw Lord Sidmouth that evening, she was determined to get him to talk to her. When he asked her for a dance, she told him she was tired and asked him if he would accompany her outside, where they might find a place to sit and talk. She was shocked at her own boldness, especially when she saw the expression in his eyes. He probably thought she was flirting with him. Well, let him.

The evening was warm and both were happy to be outside. Kate was relieved to see other couples, since she hardly wanted to place herself in a compromising position.

"There is a bench just around the corner," said Harry. "Shall we see if it is occupied?"

This would take them out of the sight of the rest, but Kate agreed.

"You are looking very pretty tonight, Miss Kate. That color green brings out the flecks of green in your eyes," he said, leaning a little closer than she was comfortable with.

"Thank you, Lord Sidmouth." It was the easiest, most practiced sort of compliment, although the first he had given her. It meant nothing, she told herself. "I hear that you accompanied my aunt this afternoon. What was that like?"

"Despite her size and age, your aunt is a formidable and admirable woman."

"Yes, Aunt Kate looks like the last person one would find in a brothel."

Lord Sidmouth laughed.

"Oh, dear, that did not come out quite the way it should have. But you know what I mean."

"I do."

"But you will say no more about your experience?"

"What I would have to say is not fit for a young woman to hear."

"Come now, my lord, I am not one of your just-out-of-the-schoolroom misses, and you have not treated me like one before now."

Well, that was certainly true, thought Harry. He had not used any of his tried and true techniques to get her alone with him. And yet, here they were alone because *she* had asked him, he realized with amusement. In the past he would have viewed it as a perfect opportunity to steal a kiss. Instead, he treated her seriously.

"I am, of course, familiar with some places in the city

that a young woman would not be. But I do not frequent St. Giles streets, nor go slumming like some of my contemporaries. So to some degree, what I saw was new to me. It is one thing to know that young girls are selling themselves. Quite another to meet one, I assure you."

"And what do you think of my aunt? Do you hold the common opinion that she should be preaching remorse and repentance to these girls?"

"I can think of nothing more ridiculous than preaching goodness to the desperate. Where would a fourteen-year-old girl who is already ruined go? How would she eat? No, your aunt is helpful in the only way she can be—by trying to make a miserable life a little less miserable. She saved one poor girl today. Of course, 'save' is a relative term," admitted Harry with a laugh.

"What do you mean?"

"She got her away from selling herself on the street and risking being beaten or worse and into a clean well-run brothel."

"And you think the girl better off?"

"Absolutely. The proprietress, Mrs. Spencer, seems a good businesswoman. She probably treats her girls decently to keep good, steady customers. I think she may even have a heart despite her commitment to profit."

"It is very easy to forget all of this when we are safe in Yorkshire," said Kate softly.

"Surely young women are ruined there, too?"

"We do have an occasional scandal," Kate admitted. "We had Peggy Metcalfe."

"And who is she?"

"A Hawes woman who ran away from her husband and child to go off with a soldier."

"And you've already told me of the infamous milkmaids of Jervaulx," teased Harry.

Kate looked up at him and smiled. "You have an impressive memory, Lord Sidmouth."

"I do. For instance, I remember everything about my visit to Yorkshire."

"Well, we will all be back there soon for the wedding. I

am sure you could find a willing milkmaid, my lord." Kate had pursued the jest without thinking and was surprised to see the look in Sidmouth's eyes.

"Is that what you think of me, Miss Kate? That I heartlessly pursue women? Although what else would you think," he continued almost to himself, "after this spring."

Without thinking, Kate put her hand on his arm. "I am sorry, Lord Sidmouth. I spoke too quickly. My opinion of you has changed over these past weeks. And I blamed you unfairly about Lynnie, which perhaps I have never fully apologized for."

"I cannot really explain my behavior away, Miss Kate. Except to say that when I came home from the war, I wanted to keep my heart from being touched and so I pursued only young women who had not the slightest chance of doing so."

"Truly, you need not justify yourself to me, Lord Sidmouth," protested Kate. She was amazed at how a thoughtless comment had wounded him.

"I do, if I wish you to know me better than you have." Harry's voice was low and serious, and Kate was surprised at how the intimacy of his comment and his tone made her feel. To hide it, she responded brightly, "Yes, well, given your friendship with Lord Clitheroe, we will be almost family."

"I suppose we will," said Harry, pulling back. Kate was both relieved and disappointed. "We had better get inside," he continued, "or people will start gossiping."

43

Although they were never alone together again, Kate felt that something had changed in Lord Sidmouth's manner with her. He seemed more relaxed and less apt to converse with her only superficially. Over the next few weeks he continued to ask her to dance, and often when James called for Lynette for a walk or a drive, Sidmouth came with him to escort Kate. And since the betrothed couple was often in their own little world, the marquess and she got to know each other better by necessity.

They found themselves telling family stories and amused one another with anecdotes from childhood.

"And have you always been the practical Richmond?" quizzed the marquess one afternoon during a walk in the park, after Kate had told him how she was always the one to come up with some way to avoid punishment for their childhood scrapes.

"Neither Gareth or I had an all-consuming interest like my parents or Lynette. We are both more down-to-earth. Perhaps a little dull, compared to the rest of the family," said Kate with a laugh.

"It is not at all fair to yourself to turn your strength into a weakness, Miss Richmond. Families always need balance."

"I suppose you are right. Look at James and Lynette."

"Yes, look at them," said Harry with a smile, taking her literally.

The other couple had stopped at the end of the path and were talking earnestly, face-to-face, hands clasped. From time to time James would lean down and drop a kiss on

Lynette's forehead or mouth. They were clearly oblivious of their companions.

"Oh dear," said Kate.

"We could turn back and assume that they will eventually follow."

"They are more likely to forget our existence. In fact, it seems they already have," said Kate dryly, as she and the marquess turned and retraced their steps.

"Will you be lonely when your sister leaves?" asked Lord Sidmouth suddenly.

"I think I will be a little," admitted Kate.

"Will you come down to London again for the Season?"

"I hadn't thought much about it," she replied. "Perhaps in the spring, since Lynnie and James will be here."

"I am glad to hear that, Miss Kate. An attractive young woman such as yourself should not be shut away in Yorkshire with no prospects."

Kate felt her heart sink down into her half-boots. The marquess sounded so politely interested. Surely if he really cared for her, he would not be encouraging her husband-hunting for another Season.

"I appreciate your concern, Lord Sidmouth," she answered coolly. "I think I hear James and Lynette behind us. If we wait here, they will catch up with us."

Harry went home from that excursion pleased to have discovered that Kate would most likely return to London in the spring, but frustrated by his seeming inability to present himself as a suitor. The more time he spent with her, the more he wanted. He hoped that his time with the family in August would help him find a way to break down the barrier that held him back from outright wooing.

The Richmonds left the city earlier than most of Society, bringing the dowager marchioness with them so she would not have to travel up alone.

When they reached home, settled themselves back in, and began preparations for the wedding, Kate found herself becoming more and more irritated with her family. Mr.

Richmond was completely absorbed by writing his account of what he had seen at Padstow. When Lynette wasn't helping him, she was mooning around in a very un-Lynette-like way, thought her sister. Lady Elizabeth was busy making up for the time she had spent away from the farm, traipsing out every day from one pasture to another, making sure the flocks had prospered in her absence. They all contributed to the wedding plans, but basically the practical details were left in Kate's capable hands. She was grateful for the dowager's presence, for her aunt was the only one willing to give her undivided attention to the wedding.

Granted, it was not to be a large or very formal occasion. The Otleys would attend and the Marquess of Sidmouth, of course. And then there were the local families. But where flowers were to come from was no small consideration in Yorkshire, and accommodations for their London guests needed to be planned. Richmond House was a good-size house, but not large enough to hold all of their guests and Kate had to make arrangements for those not in either immediate family.

By the week of the wedding Kate's mood had deteriorated even more. Her family could not seem to understand that, small or not, a wedding to which a bishop had been invited needed to be carefully planned. Much as she loved her sister and rejoiced in her happiness, there were times when she wanted to shake her. Kate's queries about last-minute details were dismissed by a gentle wave of the hand and the observation that she would have been happy to run away with James in only her shift.

When James and Harry arrived, they were shown to their rooms by a very tired and disgruntled Kate. Even the sight of the marquess's handsome face did nothing to alleviate her mood.

Harry, however, was delighted to be back with the Richmonds. The door had been opened by Lynette, as it had the first time, with Kate not far behind. This time, Miss Richmond's beauty had no effect on him. He had grown accustomed to it. All he could think was: Let James have his angel. I want my Kate. For when an obviously distracted

Kate joined her sister in greeting them, Harry looked at her and could only wonder where he had been that first time. Had he been so restless, so driven, that he had been blind to the just-rightness of Kate Richmond with her springy brown curls and honest gray eyes?

Unfortunately she had excused herself as soon as she had got them settled, and Harry quickly guessed that the full burden of the wedding had fallen on her capable shoulders. He felt immediately protective and wanted nothing more than to enfold her in his arms. He had never before felt such a rush of compassion for a woman. Desire, yes. Admiration. But never the impulse to give anything beyond his name and his airy charm. He realized that he wanted to give himself to Kate Richmond, a gift he had never before been capable of offering.

But despite his attempts to help over the next two days, he could not get her to take him seriously. The Otleys had arrived and must be settled. Gareth and Arden were late. Was it possible they had had a carriage accident? The flowers that the squire had promised from his greenhouse had not arrived either and when would she ever have time to decorate the church?

The marquess suggested, Aunt Kate urged, and Janie bullied, but Kate would not stop for a second. No, she did not need a walk, she was getting enough exercise, thank you. She was not tired, and even if she was, she would have plenty of time to sleep after the wedding.

It was not just what needed doing that kept her going. The truth was, she wanted no time to pay attention to the pain in her heart. Once James arrived, and she again saw all the small gestures of affection between him and her sister, she wanted only to lose herself in the preparations for the occasion and forget what the occasion was. For the moment she saw the marquess at the door, she knew. At some point, she knew not exactly when, she had given her heart to him. And as far as she could see, he didn't want it. Oh, he politely offered to help her out, but any gentleman would have. And so she did her best to exhaust herself and succeed quite well, falling into bed each night and waking early from a sleep blessedly without dreams.

The wedding day was clear and sunny. In her pale-blue silk, Lynette was a breathtaking bride. Even the Otleys had to admire James's choice.

"You would never guess she is a bluestocking," Lady Clitheroe whispered to the bishop.

Janie had outdone herself on the wedding breakfast. And after several toasts had been made to the bride and groom, Gareth tapped the side of his glass, and smiling broadly, said he wished to make an announcement.

"It has become obvious that our trip to Cornwall was more than successful," he said with a mischievous grin. "Here we have a most handsome and happy couple, whose first kiss came about because of the wee 'oss. And Arden and I . . . well, we should be parents by February."

Lady Elizabeth embraced her daughter-in-law, and Lynette stole a glance at James and blushed. She hoped they would very soon be making the same announcement.

Kate's throat tightened as she added her congratulations. The family had begun to wonder about an heir, though two years was not really a very long time to wait.

Aunt Kate, who was sitting next to her, slipped an arm around her niece's waist and whispered, "And what of you, my dear? As someone told me at Padstow, according to the tradition, you will be married by Christmas."

"Oh, I hardly think that is likely, Aunt Kate."

"Don't be too sure, my dear. Don't be too sure."

44

K ate awoke early the next morning. Although the wedding was over and James and Lynette started on their trip to his estate in Yorkshire for the beginning of their life together, she couldn't sleep in. Her tiredness was the nervous sort which kept one up late and awake early. After quietly getting dressed and going down to the kitchen for a quick cup of tea, she slipped out the door, hoping that a long tramp up the fell would relax her.

It was another clear, sunny day, but cool. Kate had knotted an old shawl around her shoulders, but wished she had worn her cloak. Soon, however, she was warmed up from her exertion, and as the sun got higher, she slipped the shawl off and tied it around her waist.

She passed Gabriel on the way up and waved, but did not stop. She smiled to herself at the memory of the old shepherd dressed in his best for the wedding and inviting Lady Otley to dance. She thought James's mother might have palpitations, but she redeemed herself, since Otleys were always polite and never knowingly offended the lower class. She kindly declined Mr. Crabtree's invitation by telling him she had an arthritic hip.

"Na then, lass, tha can't be much older than me. Coom on, I'll go easy on ye."

Harry had been standing behind Lady Otley and caught Kate's eye just as she was successfully choking down her laughter at the expression on Lady Otley's face. "Lass!" "Can't be much older than me!" He grinned at her and she had to excuse herself immediately. She hurried over to where her brother and Arden were chatting with the vicar, and helpless with laughter, tried to explain what had set her off.

Now why did she have to think of Sidmouth just now. They had shared a moment of amusement, and she had felt closer to him then than at any other time in their acquaintance. Damn the man. It was easier to ignore charm and handsomeness than it was a shared sense of the ridiculous.

When she reached the top, she sat down and leaned her back against one of the rocky outcroppings. A curlew called above her, a hawk floated lazily past and the sun warmed her face. Before she knew it, she was asleep.

Harry was down early, too, thinking he would be alone at the breakfast table, only to find Gareth there before him.

"I hope Lady Arden is not too tired from yesterday."

"She is fine," replied Gareth. "But I have heard that women who are breeding have a greater need for sleep in the early months."

Janie had been given the morning off, so Harry helped himself to a simple breakfast of toast, tea, and cheese.

"I am sorry we don't have more to offer you," apologized Gareth.

"After yesterday's feast, this is more than enough," replied Harry with a smile.

A little later the rest of the family joined them, and all chatted easily about the wedding. Harry kept glancing up toward the door, expecting Kate to come down any minute, but the only one who came through was the cat, who stalked over to Lady Elizabeth and jumped on her lap.

"I am sure I don't understand why you allow that animal such freedom," said Aunt Kate.

" 'Allow' is hardly the appropriate word," answered her sister-in-law with a smile. "Mott does what he wishes. Always has, haven't you, old cat?" Mott stretched out as his mistress scratched behind his ears.

"Where do you think Kate is, my dear?" Mr. Richmond asked.

"Enjoying a well-deserved rest, I hope," said Gareth.

"She worked hard enough for two people from what Arden and I could see."

When a half hour went by and still no Kate, Lady Elizabeth went up herself to her daughter's door.

"She is not asleep at all," she announced when she returned to the breakfast room. "I suspect she was up before any of us and is out on the fell."

"That is just what I was thinking of doing," remarked Harry, with studied casualness. "I need to walk off the effects of that wonderful feast. I'll keep an eye out for Miss Richmond, shall I?" And he excused himself from the table a few minutes later, eager to be off.

"You are sitting there grinning like Mott when he has caught a mouse and dropped it at Mother's feet, Aunt Kate," said Gareth after Harry had taken his leave. "Will you let us in on whatever has so amused you?"

"Later, my dear. Later."

It *was* good to be outdoors and he *did* need to work off yesterday's celebration, thought Harry as he climbed. When he came to Gabriel's hut, he decided to see if Kate had perhaps stopped for a visit.

"Good day to tha, lad," said the old shepherd.

"Good morning, Gabriel. I see you are no worse for wear this morning."

"I have a good head for t'drink, lad. Although t'cake Janie made was more like to do me in. I am not used to such food."

"Have you seen Miss Richmond this morning?"

"Oh, aye, t'lass passed by here at least an hour ago."

"Was she headed straight up the fell?"

"Aye, lad. Straight up to the top, I wager."

"Thank you, Gabriel. Her family was a little worried about her being tired from yesterday and I thought I'd make sure she is all right," explained Harry.

"T'lass will be fine. No danger of snowstorms today!" replied the old shepherd with his raspy laugh.

"Umm, no, it didn't look like bad weather was coming. I just thought she shouldn't be out too long on her own."

Gabriel dug his elbow into Harry's side. "I think I know what tha'rt thinking, lad. But just tha remember: Benjamin and I are here if Miss Kate needs us. Tha better be courting in earnest or it will be my staff in tha belly."

Harry blushed for one of the few times in his adult life. "I have the greatest respect for Miss Richmond, Mr. Crabtree. As for courting, well, she has given me no sign that she would welcome it."

"What sign does tha need, lad? I could feel what was between tha yesterday, and see the way tha was looking at each at t'other. Tha'rt a little too handsome for my liking, but Miss Kate needs someone of her own, and tha'll do."

"Thank, you, Gabriel, I think," Harry replied dryly, and continued his climb.

He saw her right away, sound asleep against the rock. She looked so relaxed and so comfortable that he did not have the heart to wake her immediately, even though he knew she would get stiff and sore from lying on the damp ground. And so he sat himself down next to her, and like Kate, gave in to the sun and fell asleep.

45

K ate had been dreaming. In her dream she was back on the bench in the garden and Harry had drawn her head down on his shoulder. His shoulder felt so solid that she allowed herself to let go of all her worries about the accounts, the housekeeping, worries she always carried with her, and enjoyed the sensation of being taken care of. The dream was so vivid that not only could she feel the texture of his coat, but also smell his cologne. The hardness of the rock against her back woke her, however, and she was prepared for the sense of longing that follows that sort of dream when she became conscious that her head was indeed on Lord Sidmouth's shoulder. She had turned a little in her sleep and there he was.

She lifted herself very carefully and looked at him. She wanted to grab his arm and pillow her head against it again, and it was very hard to resist the temptation, because how often did one's dreams become reality?

But what on earth was he doing next to her? And should she leave him or wake him? Remembering what had happened the last time, she was inclined to get up and leave quietly. But it was too hard to pull herself away.

His sleep couldn't have been that deep, because as if he felt her gaze on him, he opened his eyes and looked straight into hers. Without hesitating an instant, he turned and pulled her toward him and kissed her. As his kiss went from tentative to urgent and she responded, he abruptly let her go and pulled himself away.

Kate thought she would die from the disappointment. And then she looked at his face.

"Please, Lord Sidmouth, what is it?"

"I should not have done that."

"You may be right, but I am glad you did," replied Kate shamelessly.

He did not seem to hear her, because he was somewhere else. Kate remembered what he had said to her aunt and tried to think of something that would draw him back.

"You seemed to be enjoying the kiss, my lord," she said, pulling at his sleeve to gain his attention. "Then, all of a sudden, you seemed to go somewhere else. I hardly think one kiss, however enjoyable, would be that threatening. I will not cry compromise, I promise," she added, trying to tease him out of his distraction.

He really looked at her then.

"What are you seeing, Lord Sidmouth? Is it a memory from the war? Perhaps it is time you told someone about it."

"What I see in those moments I am thrown back to Badajoz is not something any young lady should know about."

"But it is all right for you to bear it alone? You are strong enough then to keep it to yourself? I think not, Lord Sidmouth. We are not very apart in age, you know. Had I been a man I would have seen what you did. Are we so different that you should have some sort of strength that I don't? I have often thought that we expect men to survive horrors as if they were not truly human. I have read enough to know that Badajoz was a slaughterhouse," she continued softly. "It must have been terrible to see your friends cut down."

"It was, Miss Richmond. We crawled over mines and spikes. The men were using dead and wounded bodies to make a bridge. They were even pushing their comrades onto swords, just to make it over the barricade. You cannot imagine the sight and the smells . . ." Harry shuddered as he remembered the combined smell of burning flesh and blood. "But it is not those memories, my dear Kate," he said ironically.

"Was it being wounded? You must have thought yourself near death."

Harry got up and turned his back to Kate. Looking off over the scree, he began to speak slowly, as if every word were an effort: "I was not wounded at Badajoz, Miss Richmond."

"I don't understand."

"Oh, I was, if you are speaking geographically. But not during the siege. I survived the carnage without a scratch. I made it over the bodies of the dead and dying into the city. And, I must confess, I felt no worse about it than any other battle," he added ironically.

"Then how were you wounded?"

"I doubt that the public thinks much about the behavior of men after a battle, Miss Richmond. There is something about being caught up in both fear and bloodlust at the same time that gets to men. In fact, there seems to be something about killing that is akin to . . . desire. Our men had been through hell and yet only seemed to want to create more . . . To be brief, I came upon two men raping two women, two nuns. One, I would guess was over sixty. The other, a novice, by her veil, looked about sixteen. The older one was already dead, you see, Miss Richmond. But the men were still hard at work, as it were," said Harry, not seeing the green grass in front of him, but the blood-soaked white veil that had been ripped off a young girl's head, revealing short-cropped black hair—and the habit drawn up over her knees, and the grunting of the men, like the pigs they were, as they thrust another sort of weapon into her again and again.

Harry had recounted his story in a dull monotone, and at first Kate could not take it in. It was too horrible and a part of her went numb as she heard it.

"I ordered them to stop, and they only laughed at me and said 'All's fair in love and war.' When I tried to pull them off, one stuck his bayonet in me. The other one shot me. But I was lucky, for some of my company were behind me, and they killed the two and carried me off to the surgeons."

Kate was still unable to apprehend it. Lord Sidmouth—it could have been Gareth—had seen something so far beyond her experience that she couldn't find any words of comfort. She wanted to go over and put her arms around him, but was afraid of what he might think.

"So you see, Miss Richmond, I have seen what men can become. When I came home, I tried to forget, to drive the memories out by mindless pursuit of women with whom I knew I would never experience real desire. You were right about me, my dear Kate," he added quietly.

Kate had tears in her eyes at last. She may not have been there, but she could feel his pain right here, in the present.

"Lord Sidmouth . . ." she said hesitantly.

Harry turned and looked at her. "I saw *King Lear* this spring," he said, as though commenting upon the weather. "I knew how the old man felt, his world empty of any meaning, everything and everyone tainted. How can one believe in love in such a world."

Kate knew that nothing she could say would change things. She would have to take the risk herself, and show him his own heart again, hoping she was right about the passion she had felt in his kiss. She stood up and walked over to him. Placing her hands on his shoulders, she said, "Please kiss me again, Harry."

He only looked at her bleakly, and so she reached up and ran her thumb down the side of his cheek and over his lips. He took a ragged breath, and she felt a delightful hunger rising from deep inside her. She lifted her face and at the same time grasped his hands and pulled him down on his knees in front of her. His arms tightened around her convulsively, and she felt him begin to sob.

"Oh, my dearest," she said, and held his dark head to her breast, enfolding him in her arms and letting him cry out in the privacy of her embrace.

After a few minutes the shuddering stopped, and he lifted his head. She gave him no time to think, and kissed him with infinite tenderness, wishing with all her heart she could wipe out the last two years with her love, or at least transform them. This time he responded. He kissed her tentatively at first, and then more and more recklessly. Within a few moments they were stretched out on the grass, and she was surprised and even a little frightened by her reac-

tion. She wanted him to open her dress and lower the top
and caress her breasts, and he did, as though he had read
her mind. She wanted him to take her hand and lead it
down to where she could feel the evidence of his desire,
and he did. His tongue caressed one of her breasts, circling
the nipple lazily, and Kate felt a melting between her legs.
As he reached up under her skirt, she whispered, "Wait,"
and pulled off her underthings and let him push back her
skirt. He groaned with pleasure as he buried his face in her
belly, and moved lower.

Her hand found him again, and she moaned a little in
frustration when she realized his pants were in the way.
Turning away briefly, he pulled down his breeches and
turned back. At first she was too shy to look, but then she
lifted her eyes and watched him kneeling over her. He lowered himself and stroked her skin with the shaft that was so
soft and so hard at the same time. He began with his finger
to make her ready for him, and continued by rubbing the tip
of his phallus against her until she thought she would die
from the pleasure. "Now, Harry, please, now," she murmured.

He knew he would hurt her this first time, and so he went
slowly. But she arched herself against him and pushed up-
ward as he carefully moved down, and then he was inside
her. As he began to thrust, he had one moment of panic, as
the movement brought back memory, but then he was conscious only of the present. He cupped his hands under her
head and gently rode her. And after his climax, before he
pulled himself out, he rolled her over on top of him and
reaching his finger between her legs, brought her the ec-
stasy he'd been promising.

Kate was all liquid. Had she been truly water, she would
have just flowed down over Harry, over the fellside, giving
her innermost self to him, to the grass, the ground, to everything. He had filled her to overflowing, and she felt that she
could never be empty again.

"Oh, God," he groaned as he rolled over and grabbed her
to him. "I love you so much and look what I have done to
you." But he didn't say it despairingly, although she knew

he was sorry. There was the same exultation in his voice that she felt.

"And I love you, Harry Lifton," she said and smiled into his face, daring him to regret a second.

A look of wonder crossed his face. "You do?"

"And does tha think I roll around t'fell with just anyone! I was t'one to kiss first, and tha remember that, lad!"

"That is true, and thank God you did. For I was far too frightened to do it. But then, it was like being taken over by . . . I don't know what."

"Joy and hunger."

"Yes. And I have been wanting you since Padstow. It is strange, isn't it? That whole day was about desire, and union, pure and clean and not dirtied by violence. It helped me believe a little in myself again. When I returned to London, it was as though a fever had broken. I no longer felt driven to pursue undesirable young women."

"Nor pursue me!"

"Because every bit of my so-called natural as breathing charm deserted me whenever I was close to you, Miss Kate Richmond."

"And why was that, do you think?"

"Because from the moment I saw you emerge from under the 'oss, I knew I wanted you and was terrified I could hurt you."

"Only *wanted* me?" asked Kate with a small shiver.

Harry pulled her closer. "Loved you," Harry answered simply. His hands began to wander again and in a few moments he was as hard as he had been a short while ago. This time their lovemaking was more leisurely, and even more pleasurable, for this time they had both fully taken in the fact that each loved and was loved in return.

Although the sun was warm, there was still a cool breeze, and after lying entwined for a few minutes, they both began to feel cold. Harry helped Kate with the tapes of her dress, and she looked away as he pulled up his breeches and stuffed his shirt into them.

"It is lucky you pushed my skirt up, Harry," said Kate,

for she had realized during their second lovemaking that the stickiness on her thighs came from blood as well as from him. Harry ran his hand through her curls and caressed the nape of her neck. "I am sorry to have forgotten what this meant for you, Kate."

"Don't be sorry for anything. I am not."

"Do you know what someone in Padstow told me?" he asked her as they made their way down the hill.

"What?"

"That if a young woman comes out from under the 'oss with soot on her face and tar on her arms, she will be married by Christmas."

"Oh?" said Kate, very innocently.

"I do not think that we should let the 'oss be proved wrong, do you?"

"Perhaps not, Harry."

"*Perhaps* not! You had better marry me, Miss Kate Richmond," he demanded, grabbing her around the waist. "Or Gabriel will have my head."

"I would, Harry, but I don't think I can stand the thought of another wedding!" she answered, teasing him.

"I promise you will not have to lift a finger, my dear."

"Then the sooner the better," Kate replied.

As they walked down the path, arms around each other's waist, they were oblivious to their surroundings. Gabriel saw them go by, and turning to Benjamin, said happily, "Well, I guess we did reet in rescuing those two this February, eh, lad?" And when he found Kate's abandoned shawl on the scree the next day, he just smiled and folded it up and placed it in the basket by the fire, and was not at all surprised when another wedding was announced for late September.

MEP